REVⓄLUTIⓄN:

A STⓄRY ⓄF THE FAMILY CULT ⓄF HUMBLE, TEXAS

Thomas J. Moore, Jr.

PublishAmerica
Baltimore

First printing

ISBN: 1-4137-5576-3
PUBLISHED BY PUBLISHAMERICA, LLLP
www.publishamerica.com
Baltimore

Printed in the United States of America

This book is dedicated to all of the children I met learning to read at Mrs. Curtis' round table of reading. May they continue to read, and to thank the teachers that taught them to do so.

I want to say thank you to my wife Debbie, who has been a light through the storms of our life together. And to my sons, Trace, Danny, and Sammy, who make my life brighter when they are around. Big thanks to my mother and father, Jean and T.J. Moore, for bringing my sister, Sheryl, my brother, John, and me to such a wonderful place to grow up.

Chapter I

I t may be presumptuous of me to say this, but I think anyone who has had to move into a small town would agree, it doesn't matter how long you live there, you will always be considered "the new guy."

Small towns are clannish, and as so, they shun new people who threaten to invade the personal business and private recreational activities of the town's people. There are always a few newcomers in these small towns, who out of ignorance to the close-knit kinsmen of the area and the enchantment of a new vista, buy a sliver of land and erect a house to call home. But the layers of native inhabitants (if that is the proper way to refer to people who have roots deep in the history of the village that are not necessarily aboriginal in ethnicity) are related to each other down through the decades, as people from these places tend to stay in the hometown. The inner circle, deep inside the layers of relatives, consists of the town's founding family, either immediate or distant. When I say distant, that's by an "outsider's" definition. Family is family in the small town.

That is the way I found Humble, Texas, in the fall of 1963, close knit and not readily receptive to newcomers. But if you were not "blood kin" the townsfolk may still adopt you as long as you had given your heart to Jesus and were active in one of the local church families. However, if a person didn't get up on Sunday morning and go to church, there was obviously something wrong with them. Perhaps they were some ungodly heathen or a Communist, for God's sake. I, unfortunately, was not a churchgoer when I moved to Humble, and as it turned out, it added to my inability to feel accepted by some of the other kids. I'm not saying I was a total outcast. There were others there who had moved in before and after I did. I had a lot of friends and some were even "Humble blood", but there was still a feeling—a vibe—that was always felt from the time I arrived in Mrs. Curtis' third grade class until I graduated from Humble High School on a spring evening in 1973. Reunions bring back a flood of those memories and not all are pleasant.

The first time my parents brought my younger sister, my baby brother, and me from south Houston to our new home, it was a cool autumn afternoon. At the time, it seemed like the car ride took all day. The land along the highway was not yet developed commercially as it is now. The George W. Bush Intercontinental Airport, or Jetero as it was to be called originally, had not yet been built, and construction on it would not even begin for several more years. The small tallow trees of Houston gave way to the towering loblolly pines as we neared what would be, what I consider now, my hometown.

I enrolled in Humble Elementary, the little school, during the first week in December of '63. I was actually supposed to have enrolled at the end of the month in November, before Thanksgiving, but there was that nasty business in Dallas that week. Besides, there was still some painting my parents had to do to sell the house in Houston, and there was no one in Humble my siblings and I could stay with.

On the occasion that I did start school in Humble, my mother led me by the hand to the third grade classroom of Mrs. Curtis, who was in the middle of her reading class. Mrs. Curtis seemed to me to be a very old, skinny lady with gray hair and wrinkles. She was not especially cheerful looking, which would have been a little more comforting to a small child, who had just been uprooted from the suburban area of south Houston and thrown headlong into a strange, new environment.

The reading class consisted of a large round table surrounded by children sporting, for the most part, pageboy or flat top haircuts, depending on gender. All of these children were learning to read by means of the "Dick and Jane" readers. These people, many of who are my friends today, were of varying degrees of couth. In the same proportion, they spoke in a heavy south Texas drawl, which further added to my anxiety. The school they were attending did not place emphasis as strongly on diction or manners as did the school I was moving from. So, if you can imagine being brought in and standing in front of the class to be introduced to the teacher and the class by the principal, who said:

"Mrs. Curtis, this is your new pupil, Richard Stevens," Mr. Solomon said, giving me a slight push forward toward the geriatric instructress.

"Richard, I am very glad to meet you. How are you?" she asked, shaking my hand in as much of a friendly, welcoming manner as I believe she was able.

And I, an eight-year-old, drawing from the education I had received at Williams Elementary School in Pasadena, Texas, answered as confidently as I could, "Very well, thank you."

The room instantly exploded into laughter. I had duly marked myself for the rest of my days in the Humble School District as "a little gentleman". Being labeled as such, I was not always received kindly by the good old boys around town because, I suppose, they thought that a gentleman assumes he is somewhat above them in the evolutionary ladder. My induction into the third grade class is a memory that makes me cringe every time I think about it. My wife, Debbie, who was present that day at the reading table and participated in the belly laughing and at the time, still gets a kick out of reminding me of that painful moment. Well, there is a saying that goes, "If you don't give people something to talk about they'll just make something up." I can testify that there were at least twenty-five less liars in the school that week.

In 1963 the population of Humble (which is pronounced with a silent H) was less than perhaps 2,000 people. Many were farmers, others commuted to work in Houston, and others worked the few remaining oil wells that were still producing.

In the much earlier history of Humble, it started as a sawmill town, and then oil was discovered in 1904. As an oil boomtown, the countryside became freckled with wooden oil derricks more numerous than there were dwelling places. It's the place Humble Oil and Refining Company was named after. While drilling one of the wells in 1912, an underground river was tapped into, producing an artesian well in Humble that flows to this day at the corner of North Houston Avenue and 1st Street.

In another area of town called Moonshine Hill (named after the custom of the former inhabitants of distilling smooth alcohol on a frequent basis) quite a few bad boys of the oil boom days gathered for nights of drinking, fighting, kissing a pretty woman, and playing a little poker. Oil production in Humble began in the 1910s drawing as many as 10,000 people to the area. The hill was in close proximity to the oil patch and was on the outskirts of town. Many shootouts took place among those wildcatters who could not settle a disagreement any other way. Partaking in the namesake of the vicinity only added to their recklessness. It was a time when, as they say, "the derricks were made of wood, and the men were made of steel".

However, by the time I arrived that was all very much ancient history, and this recollection does not really depend on the history of the town. The fact that it was a small town is all that needs to be said. It consisted of a main street, named accordingly, on which there was a five and dime store, a barber shop, a bank, a theater, hardware store, etc., and one more street of commercial enterprises affording a grocery store, a dry cleaners, and a couple of gas stations. In all, the small town near the San Jacinto River contained the businesses that, of course, make up a town.

In any of those places of business, after we had lived there for a few years, we knew, or at least were familiar with, almost everyone. And that was a good thing, I suppose. It was, from time to time, a bad thing for a teenage adolescent like me. In a place like that you can't sport sinful ways and expect to get away with it. If one were to take up smoking or run with a fast girl it was sure that the parents would find out in no time. This is the voice of experience talking here.

The town had its fair share of people who might be considered anything from local celebrity to the town character. A favorite celebrity of mine was a former teacher I had while attending Charles Bender Junior High School. His name was Bevel Jarrell, a history teacher and former football coach. Actually, I believe he founded football in Humble. I'm not positive about that statement, but I do know he was the one who dubbed the junior high football team with a nickname they used for many years. It was during the time when

Humble was a very poor school district. They couldn't afford nice uniforms for the senior high team, much less the junior high. The junior high team was using the old battle weary uniforms of the high school that were on the way to the dump when someone decided they were still good enough for the little kids. When the boys donned the newly acquired, though threadbare, uniforms, Coach Jarrell came out for practice, took a good look at his young rag-tag team and speculated, "Well, if y'all don't look like the biggest bunch of Bo Diddles I ever saw." From then until someone recently decided that it was a vulgar moniker for their brave little lads in purple and white, the junior high team was called the Humble Bo Diddles.

On the other hand, there was the town drunk, John Nell. He was quite helpful at directing traffic when school let out. He would stand in the middle of one of the street crossings, smashed to the gills, flagging cars, busses, and children crossing the street, while trying to maintain his balance. He sometimes had a bit of a problem with gravity when he was in his usual condition. There were other times he helped the basketball referees keep the game straight by getting right out on the floor during the game, and you know, just lending a friendly helping hand. Some friends and I talked with him one evening at the city park. He had his three dogs with him, and he told us that those three dogs were worth a hundred dollars apiece to him. We were amazed. That was a lot of money to a teenager in the early '70s. I didn't know what he meant at the time. They were just some old mutt dogs. A few years later it dawned on me—he was counting them off on his income tax. Dependants were worth one hundred dollars each at the time and did not require a social security number. We won't even talk about the night he took a big bite out of a live duck at the Humble Rodeo.

So, there it is. Humble in the '60s and '70s was a very small, close-knit, relatively quiet town with a few notable characters. The big city lights were twenty miles away, and that's the way we liked it. No hustle and bustle. If ever there was a traffic jam it would have had to have been caused by a few cows running loose on Old River

Road or at Three Mile Bend. The kind of race riots the older kids participated in was out on North Belt Road to see whose car could run the quarter the quickest. Crime, except for misdemeanors, was virtually unheard of in this sleepy little burg.

In this town you would have never suspected a family like the Chase family.

CHAPTER 2

One afternoon in the band hall during my senior year, as I sat in my chair beside the other trumpet players amid the smells of cork grease and valve oil waiting for band practice to begin, I saw there in the clarinet section a vision of heaven. At that moment, everything else was totally blotted out. The screeching of reeds and the blaring of horns, the rat-a-tat-tat of drums and the droning of voices were all gone, and my full attention was given to the lady in black. How it was I hadn't noticed her before was an enigma. I knew probably ninety-nine percent of the people in the band, and how in the world I had not seen her before was an absolute mystery to me.

Hoping to be educated on her identity, I nudged the guy sitting next to me, "Allen, who is that girl over there sitting in the first clarinet section?"

"You mean Veree Currie?"

"No. I know Veree. The one sitting beside her. Who's that?"

"Susan Jenkins?"

"No, no. The other side. Is she a new girl or what?"

"Monica Dempsey?"

By this time I was annoyed, "Allen, for crying out loud, do you see anyone over there that you *don't* know?"

"Oh, yeah! Yeah, I don't know who she is."

"Well, ask Rat if he knows," I told him.

He turned and asked Rat, who turned and asked the next guy and so on until the puzzle was finally solved.

"Her name is Sylvia Chase," Alan reported. "And, yes, she moved in last week. Her family has lived here for a long time, but she's been away at school somewhere else. Do you have some valve oil I can borrow?"

I tried to keep an eye on her for the rest of the class. When she got up to leave she left with Rhonda (Humble blood) beside her. I knew Rhonda well enough, and I should have started to quiz her about Sylvia right away, but in a twelfth grade class with only 350 students total, all you have to do is mention that you have noticed someone and the word will make its way to that person.

It did.

Rhonda told me Sylvia had already been asking about me several days before.

"Oh yeah, she likes you, Rick," Rhonda told me the next day as we walked through the congested hallway to Mr. Denny's history class. "But she's not like most girls around here. As a matter of fact she's not like *anyone* around here."

"What do you mean, Ronnie?" I asked her as she dug out some notebooks from her jam-packed locker.

"She talks kinda funny, like she's above everybody. She wears black all of the time," she said. Then she cupped her hand and whispered, "She even wears black underwear." As if someone was going to brand her a strumpet for saying the word underwear to a boy. "And when we were talking the other day, I invited her to come to church with me, and she told me she already belongs to a church, but she kept talking about God like He's a *woman*," she said with a look of absolute amazement on her face.

"Well, shut my mouth, y'all! There are other religions than the main stream Protestant and Catholic churches, you know?" I said mainly just to annoy her.

"Yes, I know, and that's fine for folks who don't mind burning in hell forever. I was trying to invite her to a full gospel church, where she can get saved and full of the Holy Ghost." She slammed her locker door shut and continued, "And that's exactly what you should be doing, Ricky Stevens. Turn or burn, honey, you need to get yourself to church."

"Rhonda, babe," I said with a look of apathy, "what I need is to get myself to class. What you need is to go drink a beer sometime. Maybe that'll kill that bug up your ass."

Ouch! She stayed mad at me for the rest of the week for that one, but deep down inside I'm sure she loved me in a plutonic brotherly sort of way. She couldn't stay mad at me for very long.

The next day, after lunch, I walked outside to get a little air and to find someplace where I could sneak a smoke. It was a beautiful January day. The sky was a clear deep blue and the temperature was not bad. It was probably because the humidity was so low. Humidity on the Gulf Coast always works against you because in the summer it makes it seem hotter, and in the winter it makes it seem colder. There were only a few precious days when it's just about right, and this seemed to be one of them. It was cool enough that I had on my blue jean jacket. It was the one with the green peace symbol on the left sleeve where soldier's stripes would be. It drove the teachers and my parents crazy. There was a very unpopular war going on, you know? It was my job to be rebellious.

As I walked out of the building, I noticed my reflection in the glass door. I don't know how vain it made me, but I thought I had a really good build. I know that sounds weird, and I didn't go around telling everyone what I thought. I was just kind of proud of it. My hair was getting a little on the long side. As a matter of fact, it was touching my ears on the sides and in the back it was down to my collar. Horrors! They were pretty strict around here on how long a guy's hair could be and mine was just at the threshold. I guess I'll have to go ahead and bite the bullet and go see Mr. Gothard at the barbershop. Mr. Gothard specialized in one kind of hair cut. They were called "white walls," and white walls referred to the scalp being exposed around the ears because the hair was cut so short. I hated the short hair, but deep down in my soul I *knew* I was a hippie. It was a very groovy time to be a kid.

I had on one of my favorite pair of jeans. They were a pair of flare-legged, faded beauties, and they were broken in just right. I emphasize that they were flares because no guy in his right mind would have been caught dead around here in bell-bottoms. Any guy that would wear those surely had a little sugar in his tank, if you know what I mean. Being known as a gentleman was one thing, but anyone who might be suspected of homosexuality at this time and in this place might have reason to fear for his life.

On the high school campus there are live oaks planted. Under each one, buried in the ground in front of them, is a little plaque saying that this and that tree was planted in memory of guys that had died in World War I or II or some other life wrenching calamity. The trees provided shade from the Texas winter sun. The shade the trees provided made it nice for some of us to come out after lunch to read or talk or whatever. I saw Sylvia under one of these trees. It was the last tree on the far side of the campus. She was sitting under the tree cross-legged with her back to me. I walked up quietly behind her. I don't know why I did. I wanted to introduce myself, and at the same time I didn't want to disturb her. She was up on the fashion craze. She was wearing bell-bottoms, headband, leather vest, a pair of shades…the works. You notice I said bell-bottoms. That was what the girls wore. Strictly taboo for guys.

I walked up behind her and said, "Hi! Is your name Sylvia? I saw you in band, and I was wondering if maybe you wanted to go get a coke or something after school?"

She sat there saying nothing. Maybe I hadn't been loud enough. There are times when people say I mumble a little.

"Sylvia? I'm Ricky. How about a coke after school? You wanna go?"

"Come sit here on the ground next to me," she said, patting a place on the ground. I sat down Indian style, like her, and she continued, "Close your eyes and empty your mind."

I sat there for a few seconds trying to close out everything. "I can't…"

"Don't say that word," she said. "Think of yourself as a rock, and then try to imagine being that rock. Let your mind flow down the river."

I sat there quietly. I couldn't quite do what she wanted me to do, not that I didn't try. I was kind of interested in what she was doing and I had heard about people using meditation. After all, the Beatles and the Doors and Mia Farrow all went to India to hang out with the Maharishi, so it must be cool. But my legs were going to sleep pretty fast sitting in that position. I was really enjoying sitting next to her, though. That was the really good part. She was exceptionally fine looking.

Finally she stood up and dusted the grass off of her butt, "I like to meditate after lunch. How did you like it?"

I stood and stretched my legs to Houston and back. It felt good to get the kinks out of them. "I think I need more practice," I told her.

"Fine, I'll coach you," she said as she started to walk back to the school. She said it as if that were that. I would learn meditation and she would coach me. It was decided. So let it be written. So let it be done.

"My name's Ricky," I said, trotting up beside her. I felt like a gangly geek.

"Yes, I know. You're the soloist in the trumpet section of the orchestra. I saw you yesterday during rehearsal," again said in a deliberate emotionless way. "You have obviously excelled in your chosen art." She stopped and turned lifting her sunglasses off of her nose as she said, "That's highly admirable." She paused again for a second and then asked, "Do you feel your mind is open?"

"An open mind? In regard to what exactly?" At that point the bell rang. It was time to go back to the classrooms and get through the last half of the day. "So what about going to get a coke after school?"

"Do you drive a car?" she asked as she put her shades on top of her head.

"Well, yeah! I have a red '69 Volkswagen Bug," I announced rather proudly. All the hippies drove a Volkswagen of some kind.

"I'll meet you at the door of Mrs. Randolph's biology class right after we get out of orchestra rehearsal," she said and walked quickly through the doorway and on into the stream of people trying to get to the next class. I watched her until she vanished, and then I watched the spot where I had last seen her walking.

I went on to class with the thought that there was something that instantly clicked when I talked to her. It was the strangest first encounter I had ever experienced with a girl. I couldn't do anything the rest of the day except think of her. She smelled like a flower garden of roses and gardenias after a rain shower. Her straight, shiny hair flowed down splashing onto her shoulder, and it was the color of dark chocolate. It sparkled contrasts in the sunlight. Her lips were the color of ripe, red cherries. The most captivating thing about her appearance, though, was her unusual eyes. They were a piercing blue—almost electrified. They had a wildness about them. Her eyelashes were long and dark, and it was not from her make-up, either. Just to look at her face and the expressions she made excited me, and yes, she did talk kind of uppity.

"Hey," I felt a nudge. "HEY!"

As I looked up I saw Don Cox grinning that grin that only made me want to grin back at him. It was a goofy grin, but he was my bud. He and I had known each other almost as soon as I had moved in around the corner from him. We raised a lot of hell together.

"What are you doing, man? You zoning out on everything today?" he asked as I rose up out of my desk.

"What are you talking about?" I asked him as I worked all the kinks out of by back. Whoever designed these desk chairs was a sadistic moron—they were killers, is what I'm talking about.

"Ms. Booker asked you a question and you didn't answer. Then I came up and hollered at you twice before you came to. You didn't smoke a joint before you came in, did you?" he asked as he searched for any evidence of a buzz in my eyes.

"No, no! I was just thinking." I stood and gathered up my books. I had just finished English class and now on to biology. Yuck!

"Oh. Well, you sure work hard at thinking, then, 'cause Robert Jordan dropped a book so old lady Booker would bend over and pick it up. Her butt was eye level and two feet from your face when she went for it, and you didn't even notice. I mean, she might be almost thirty, but she don't look that bad for an old lady."

We walked out into a hall teeming with people trying to get to their next class. There were people running, slamming lockers, leaning up against walls, and some of those had their tongues rammed down someone else's throat mopping their tonsils.

The cool kids were passing by, too. There were some fine looking ladies in that crowd, and the guys always seemed like they could get away with anything. I thought that I would never fit in with that bunch, but I sure wanted to. They all lived on the north side of the river, in Forest Cove. That's where all the rich people lived. The guys had long hair, or at least it was relatively long. It was over their ears, and it touched the collar on the back of their shirts. They always wore T-shirts so the collar would be lower. And their hair was straight. If a guy had straight hair in the early '70s he was *in*! Girls too—straight hair was the rage, and all the people in this crowd had it all together.

Then I remembered Don.

"Yeah, yeah. I just get so bored in Booker's class. She wants the whole class to read at a certain pace, and I just can't do it, man. I'll be fifteen pages ahead of everyone else, and then she wants to call on me and ask me some stupid question from way back. Then when I look at her like 'what the hell are you talking about' she makes some comment that makes me look like I'm standing there fondling my cods. Oh, everybody gets a big kick outta that. Then she comes up with those retarded analogies of stories. The fish in *The Old Man and the Sea* represents the personal accomplishments in a person's life, from which is drawn personal satisfaction and worth, while the sharks are those people that would discredit and belittle the person and his or her accomplishment. The boat represents one's life being tossed about on the turbulent seas of life. *The Pearl* is a story of the selfish extent to which humanity will go to obtain and retain the material possessions it wants. How about that question on the test this morning? Is *Animal Farm* about (a) farming, (b) Communism, (c) capitalism or (d) Buddhism? Well, I reckon! Any idiot would be able to see that it's about Communism."

We were pushing our way steadily closer to the goal: my locker. It's like wading in quicksand to get through all these people, get your locker open, get the books shuffled around, and then get to the next class before the bell rings. If the bell rings, you're the goat, and the goat gets to go to D-Hall after school.

"*Animal Farm* is about Communism, huh?" Don said, raising his right eyebrow and stroking his chin thoughtfully. "I missed that one. So, what are you doing after school?"

"Why?" I asked.

"I just wanted to know if you wanted to hang out. We could go over to Rat's or Woody's and see if they've got any herbs to share."

"Nah, I'm supposed to meet someone after school. I can't," I said as I fumbled with the accumulated treasures in my locker that were in my way.

"Who?"

"Sylvia Chase."

"Don't know her. Where is she from?"

"I don't know. I'd never seen her before either." I banged my hand on my locker door and gazed in the general direction of the biology lab. "Then I saw her in band yesterday. She calls it the orchestra. Anyway, I saw her in band, and all I know about her is that she plays a clarinet and she's into meditation."

"Meditation?"

"Yeah! She's gonna teach me. But, anyway, that's what I'm doing," I said as I finally located my biology book and threw the English book in the quagmire of my locker. It was useless to try to clean it out. Besides, when would I ever get time to do that?

Two classic full-blown geeks walked by just then like some sort of wading birds looking for a quick meal of tadpoles. They had their Pocket Pal pocket protectors, horn-rimmed glasses, and their slacks looked like they were pulled up to their chest. They had that certain Alfalfa look going for them.

"Mediation, huh?" Don said, keeping one eye on the geeks. He didn't want a geek cootie jumping over and ruining his hard-earned cache of coolness. "Well, knock yer lights out. How about a ride in the morning?"

"Tomorrow's Saturday."

Don's brow furrowed, and he kind of looked up inside of his head. "Oh, yeah! You wanna hang out tomorrow?"

"I'll give you a call."

"That's cool. Later, cat." And he walked away to whatever class it was he was going to. It might have been home economics. At first, he caught hell from a lot of the guys around school, mostly the jocks and the kickers. But, all the people in the class were girls. He was the only guy in an all girl class. Not too shabby. Not too shabby at all.

But, that's how most of my day went. Zoned out thinking about Sylvia or explaining why I was zoned out.

It came time for the final class of the day—band. I got my horn and sat in my chair in great expectation of enjoying the coming treat—the entrance of Sylvia. Sylvia came in and my eyes were glued on her, but she was not even looking at me. I was trying to make eye contact with her way over there across the room in the clarinets, but she wasn't looking. Did she not feel the same thing I felt when we sat under the tree earlier? Was I just imagining that click thing? Maybe she didn't feel anything at all about me. Oh, man! If that's true how am I gonna get her to like me? Why am I so obsessed with her?

Then it happened. She looked at me. She looked at me and smiled. That class was the longest one of the day. Finally, the bell rang.

I caught up with her and reconfirmed, "You still wanna go get a coke?"

"I'll meet you in the hallway where I told you I would."

"OK.," I said and walked quickly to my locker and then to the biology lab door.

She was there.

"You ready?" I asked her.

"Absolutely, let's go," she responded.

As we walked out to my car I couldn't think of anything else to say except, "You know, ever since I laid eyes on you yesterday I haven't been able to think of anything or anyone else. Do you think that's a little strange?"

She just smiled back at me, but when we got in the car I repeated the question.

"For real. Don't you think it's odd I haven't thought of anything else but you today? I mean, I couldn't concentrate on anything."

"Well, maybe I've put a spell on you. Did you think about that?" she asked with a little grin and looking at me from the corner of her eyes.

"No," I chuckled, "I didn't think about that."

"You don't believe in such things. Is that right?"

"I've really never thought a whole lot about it. How do you stand on it?" I said as I pulled out of the school parking lot.

"While I was in the school my parents sent me to, a school for the specially gifted in New Orleans," she paused, smiled, and looked at me from the corner of her eyes, "I studied witchcraft and voodoo. I studied white and black magic, Egyptology, and the kabbalah." She giggled and I didn't know whether she was telling the truth or not. "Are you appalled?"

"Yeah, but you're kidding about putting a spell on me, right?"

"So you're saying you *are* appalled?"

"No! No! You're a very beautiful...witch, I guess...but you didn't really put a spell on me, right?"

"No, I didn't put a spell on you." She bit her bottom lip and then said, "It's very sweet of you to have a crush on me. I think you're cute, also."

"Yeah?"

"Yes, I do."

I felt like Rudolph the Red-Nosed Reindeer in that little claymation cartoon. *She said I'm c-u-t-e!*

"So, what do you do with your witchcraft?' I asked as we approached the after school hot spot of Humble—the Dairy Barn.

"Oh, just stuff. What kind of things are you interested in?" she asked as we entered. I ordered a couple of drinks and we sat down in the booth in the back.

"What am I interested in? If you mean what my long range plans are as far as college, I thought about studying to be a marine biologist. I love the ocean. In the summer I practically live in Galveston. If you just walk along the beach you see so much life. You can see seaweed, crabs, and those little clams that dig down deeper into the sand every time a wave uncovers them. Then sometimes, if you sit and watch you'll see the fish jumping out there in the waves or porpoise sounding just a few yards away. The smell of the salty sea air—it just turns me on."

"That sounds nice. We need to go there. That would be a great place to meditate," she said sipping her cherry coke.

"It's great down there in the fall and winter. There are hardly any tourists. It's too cold to get into the water, but it's nice to just be there. And you'd love the sunsets."

Then I thought she had surly been to Galveston. Hell, everyone that lives around here had been there hundreds of times, probably.

"I'm sorry." I could feel my face turning red. "You probably know the island better than I do."

"Not really. I've only been a couple of times. My family doesn't go out much," she said sheepishly.

"You're parents work a lot?"

Her eyes widened and she looked a little shaken, "What?"

I knew my face was red then. "I'm sorry. That's none of my business."

"No. That's OK. They just never have been real big on outings, that's all."

I felt like the time had come to change the subject. But that uncomfortable pause between subjects was a real obstacle. I took a long sip of my root beer float and in a sort of juvenile desperation I asked her, "So, what about you. What do you like?"

"I like to listen to classical music," she said with a look like *What you think about that?*

"Classical music?" I couldn't help but snicker. She was right. I couldn't believe it.

"Sure! I love to listen to Mozart's *Eine kleine Nachtmusik*, or the *Requiem*. Do you know what that is?"

I had to confess I didn't.

"That's Mozart's *Mass for the Dead*. I also like Beethoven's *Symphony #9*, the *Ode to Joy*. I guess my favorite composer, if I had to choose, I suppose would have to be Wagner. His music is so deep. I love his compositions like *The Ride of the Valkeries, The Flying*

Dutchman Overture, and *Elsa's Procession*. It's so triumphant," she said, swirling the ice around in her drink. "But, I like other things, too. I like cats. Do you like cats?"

"I had a cat once," I told her. "It was a Siamese we called Ms. C. My brother had a parakeet at the same time. One day we came home to find the cat had eaten the bird and boogied. We never saw it again. At least I didn't. I think my brother may have shown it the bottom of the San Jacinto River."

"So you have a brother?"

"Oh yeah, and a sister, too. Sheryl's fifteen and John's eleven." I paused for a moment. "I'm the oldest."

I was realizing how stupid that sounded when she said, "Let's see, a sister who is two years younger, and a brother who is six years younger...by gollies! You're right! You are the oldest!" She laughed.

"And I has always been good at cipherin'," I said, trying to laugh off my faux pas. When you screw up that badly, nothing helps. "You got any brothers or sisters?"

"I have one brother that's older than I am. That makes me the baby, by the way," she said as she poked me in the ribs. "I have a brother named Bruce. He's a couple of years older than I am."

We talked way into the afternoon and time got away from us. I looked at my watch and it was already a quarter to six. I knew my mom was going to yell at me for not calling.

Sylvia and I jumped into the VW and I took her to her house, which was not too far from where I lived. I was surprised that she lived in the old house off of North Belt, though. Everyone around the neighborhood had always said it was haunted.

It was a wooden frame house. Not the kind that sits up on blocks but was actually built with a basement. Very few houses in southeast Texas have a real basement being so close to sea level.

The house looked sturdy enough, but I'd heard that it was one of the oldest houses in the area—pre-Civil War. I suppose that is where the rumor of haunting came from.

The legend was that years ago an unwed mother, a girl named

Julietta Hilton of about sixteen, had given birth in this house to a little baby girl she named Bonnie Jean.

Being an unwed mother, Julietta was the shame of the family. They chastised her and treated her like she was an idiot in a real sense. They would lock her up at night in her bedroom to prevent her from wandering, and she wasn't allowed to bathe herself. One of the female house-hands had to be in the room with her and scrub her vigorously all over. She was forced to do all of the disgusting menial chores. When she wasn't tending to the baby she was to do such things as hauling the catch pan away from the outhouse and burning it clean, washing out spittoons, or killing and cleaning the evening meal—a chicken or catfish or whatever it was that had stumbled onto the menu that night.

As the story goes, Julietta soon broke down under the strain of being treated in that way. One night, in a fit of insane fury as the baby lay crying uncontrollably, she snapped, grabbed the child by the ankles, and smashed the little girl against the wall of the nursery killing her instantly. It hushed the crying of the child to all of the family except the teenage mother. She continued to hear the baby crying in every still moment she had, especially at night when she was trying to go to sleep. The family never even showed the young mother where they had laid the baby to rest, so she often broke free of her restraints and wondered the woods crying out for the child as if it would answer. One night she took a rope along with her as she ventured into the woods and put an end to her own days in the flesh. And now, so the legend goes, she wanders eternally in these woods calling out to her Bonnie Jean to answer. The only answer she ever hears is the distant crying of a wee little one who cannot be comforted.

A chill ran up my spine. I thought of that story as I let Sylvia out in the driveway up near her house. She invited me in to meet her family, but I was already in for it, so I humbly declined.

I sat there for a few seconds watching her disappear in the fading light as she walked to her door. She turned and waved, and I began to back out of the drive.

As I turned to begin backing out, a huge dog ran towards the bumper of my Bug. I slammed on the breaks to keep from hitting it, and it kept coming at a full run until it was at my window, which was down about a quarter of the way. It looked like a mad dog barking unceasingly, drooling, and snarling like it wanted to drag me out and tear me into little pieces. It never tried to get into the car. It was so big, I thought it must be half Great Dane and half Russian wolfhound. It ran off into the woods disappearing from sight. I was a little shaken up, but I got myself together, backed out, and went home.

Home was less than a mile away. It was in a neighborhood that was just a little more than five miles or so from Humble going south towards Houston. Our house was one of those that was brick half way up and then wood from there on. Mom had her rose bushes in the front flowerbed and Dad had his wood shop in the back.

He had it just for a hobby. There were some pretty cool tools out there: jig saws, band saws, a lathe, sanders. He and Sears remodeled the inside of the house because it didn't look too great when we moved in.

Like I said, it was just a hobby. He worked at a chemical plant several miles away in Channelview, Texas. He didn't actually have to go out and do what ever those guys in the hard hats and tool belts did anymore. He was hurt in an accident there when I was just a little kid, and he was burned pretty badly all over the right side of his body. A guy opened the wrong valve letting in water that was just below the boiling point, so as a settlement they put him though college and gave him a desk job watching over the maintenance guys. He made sure their time sheets got done and logged.

My sister, Sheryl, was a gangly, brown haired, green eyed, silly fifteen-year-old, who had been madly in love with Davy Jones of the Monkees until Bobby Sherman came along. Before Davy it was the guy that played Ben Casey and Kookie, the valet, from that show *77 Sunset Strip*.

My little brother, John, was just an eleven-year-old kid who knew in his heart of hearts that Batman was real, and Caesar Romero always had been and always would be the Joker.

When I walked in, mom did her bit:

"Just where the hell have you been? School was out over two hours ago! Do you know what time it is? Would it kill you to pick up a phone and call? How are we supposed to know if you're not dead in a ditch somewhere? Sometimes I wonder what it is you kids use for brains. Now go wash your hands, dinner's ready."

I knew I was gonna get *that* speech. That was *the* speech. I stood and took it like a man. I had learned to do that because years ago I actually tried to answer those questions. Then I found out it only made it worse. If she thinks you want to carry on a conversation about it she can go on forever. It's probably a woman thing to have to get the last word in.

Dad was in his usual after work position, drinking a glass of tea in his kick back chair, watching the news on the television. Just last year he finally broke down and bought a color set. I bet we were the last family in the world, or at least on the block, to get a color TV. He used to tell us if we looked at the black and white set with our eyes squinted real hard we would be able to see it in color. Personally, I never bought that theory.

After dinner I called Don. "Hey, what's happening?" I asked when he picked up.

"Not much. Your old lady called over here looking for you. Did you get the speech?"

"Oh yeah. It wasn't so bad. So, what are you doing?" I asked, knowing full well the kind of conversation I was about to have.

"Nothing. What are you doing?"

"Nothing. You wanna do something?"

"OK. What do you wanna do?"

"I don't know. What do you wanna do?"

Anyway, to make a long story short, we wound up over at a house where a couple of guys lived whom we called by animal names. I don't know how they got them, but they seemed to fit them. It was the thing back then to be called by some sort of alias. The guys we went over to see were Rat and Monkey. There were other guys around who used weird names, too. There was a guy called Snake (and he was),

Woody was named after the woodpecker cartoon character, Gorilla (Go, for short) and Bear. There were people named after inanimate objects, too. There was a guy called Buttons, one we called Bar-B-Que, and a girl named Peaches. Yeah, weird, I know!

Don and I got back to the neighborhood about ten o'clock that Friday evening. We lit a couple of cigarettes and stood in the street in the cool winter air talking for a little while.

"What are you doin' tomorrow?" he asked.

"Sylvia and I are going to the beach in the morning. She's gonna try to teach me how to meditate."

"Oh, yeah. The meditation girl. What's she like?"

"She's really kinda deep. She's into all this meditation, karma, in touch with the cosmos. But, she makes it sound interesting, so I'm gonna try it out. You know what they say, 'Don't knock it 'till you've tried it.' And, she likes to listen to classical music."

"Classical?" he laughed, flipping his cigarette butt across the street.

"That's what I said, but she says it's great. I mean, I've listened to it before too, but I don't think I could listen to it all the time."

"So, she listens to it all the time?"

"I don't know that, for sure. I had the radio on KLOL coming from Humble, and she didn't seem to *not* like it," I said as I flipped mine away. I got off the car and stretched. "I guess if she didn't like rock and roll she would have told me. I better go on in. I'll give you a holler when I get in tomorrow. You gonna be around?"

"If I'm not at the house call over to Bear's. I might be over there," he said as he crossed the street to his house.

I went in and the old folks were already in their bedroom. I found my way in the dark to my room and crashed.

CHAPTER 3

At five the next morning, (which by the way is the very butt crack of dawn), the alarm rang. I jumped out of bed, showered, shaved, got dressed, and threw on a little Hai Karate after shave. I didn't want to smell like a goat's ass, is all I'm trying to say. Besides, I might get lucky. That's every teenage guy's hope from the time they get up in the morning until they go to sleep at night. Man, it's a drag to have your hormones raging twenty-four hours a day, seven days a week, looking for a way onto the big interstate highway of love, and all the on ramps are closed until further notice. I knew it wasn't going to happen, but a man can dream, can't he?

I pulled up to Sylvia's house and she was waiting. She threw her blanket and whatever else that was into the back seat and we were off. Galveston was about an hour and a half from the house.

When she got in she looked like she wasn't quite awake yet.

"You OK?" I asked as we started down the road.

"I'm just tired. I didn't get a lot of sleep last night."

"Oh. Well, are you sure you feel well enough to go? We could make it some other time, if you want to," I offered.

"No, that's OK I'll just get a little cat nap and I'll be fine." She pulled the blanket from the back, wrapped up, and knocked out for a good while.

By the time we passed the NASA Road cut-off, the sun was just beginning to come up. It was pretty with the clouds breaking up the sunrays. It looked like one of those religious pictures that showed all the beams of light coming from behind the clouds. The moon was just about to set, too. It was just a little sliver of a crescent. The night before there hadn't even *been* a moon. Now I had the sun coming up on one side, and the moon setting on the other. Just about then is when Sylvia woke up.

"Hey, kid. Did ya sleep OK?"

"Yeah, thanks. Where are we?" she said, pushing her hair out of her face.

"We'll be going by League City here in a minute. You feel like eating breakfast?"

"Yeah, I guess. Is there a place around here?"

"There's an IHOP up here a little ways."

When we got to the restaurant we got a booth and began to examine the menu. Our waitress came to take our order, and she looked like she might have weighed about 275 on the hoof. She was a real little dumpling.

"So, what'll it be, kids?" she asked in a tone that sounded like her feet were probably killing her, and she couldn't wait to get off of them.

"I'll have the three egg omelet, bacon, and some grits. Y'all have grits, right?"

"Well, where do you think you are, sonny? This is *Texas*," the waitress replied.

"Oh, well, OK then. Since we're in Texas I'll have a bowl of grits with lots of butter and a glass of milk. What do you want, Sylvia?"

"I'll have the steak and eggs. I would like the steak very rare, and I'll a glass of milk, also."

She liked her steak rare, not just rare…*very* rare. Yes, indeed. She was not like any other girl I had ever dated.

We arrived at the beach a little after sunrise. The sky was crystal clear and the water was a dark beautiful blue. The blue-green waves were rolling, trying in vain to hold on the shore, and the whitecaps nodded and threw diamonds high into the air. Seagulls gracefully hung in mid-air on the sea breeze, and we spread out a quilted blanket in the loose sand. I slipped off my jeans and tee shirt. Underneath were my cut-offs and tank top.

"What a great day," I said. "What do you think?"

"I think this is perfect for meditating," she said, taking off her shirt revealing a crimson bikini bra. Then she shed her jeans revealing the skimpy bikini bottoms.

"I hope it doesn't get too chilly for this. I really wanted to get some sun today," she said to no one who was listening to her.

By now, my hormones had kicked in and I had to try to hide the fact that I was aroused. "OK, you come sit here," she insisted. I was sure she noticed the protrusion in my cut-offs, but she didn't say anything.

I sat down across from her on the blanket. Again, it was cross-legged which was not very comfortable, but I wasn't going to complain. The sounds of the breakers were in our ears along with the swiftly blowing wind, and the radiant winter sun was on our face.

"Let your arms hang comfortably," she began the instruction. Her hands were resting on her knees, so I put my hands on my knees, too.

She continued by saying, "If you are uncomfortable at all adjust yourself to be comfortable." I saw her glance at my crotch ginning a little grin, and I felt my face turn red. I loosened my legs a little. I had them crossed pretty tightly.

"Now, close your eyes and listen to everything around you," she went on. "Then blank them out one by one. Try to imagine what a rock is like. It sees nothing. It hears nothing. It thinks nothing. Try to be that rock."

I closed my eyes and at first everything was there. I heard the waves breaking, the gulls squealing, and the cool wind blowing across my ears. Then I tried to do what she had said. I blanked out all the sounds I could. I finally blanked them all out. Then I tried to imagine a rock. No see, no hear, no think. I felt like I was on a river floating along with the current. Then I finally did it. It was quick. I got there for just a second, and then popped out of it.

"I think I did it!" I said out loud.

"Yeah, I think you did too," Sylvia said. "I've never seen anyone do it as quick as you."

"What do you mean?" I asked.

"It's after nine o'clock. You've been meditating for over two hours. It takes most people years to get that far. You've done this before, haven't you?"

"No, really, I haven't," I said, grinning a stupid grin.

"That's amazing. You'd be a natural."

"A natural for what?"

"Well, I believe in a lot of stuff that the main stream people wouldn't understand. I don't want to scare you off."

"I'm fairly open minded about things, you know? What kind of stuff? You mean like voodoo and stuff…that witchcraft?"

"Yes, that's a part of the things I believe in, and I know not everyone can accept the belief in them. But, what are your beliefs? What do you believe is true?"

"Well, I believe in God, if that's what you mean," I began. "I don't know exactly who or what God is, but I know that there is a supreme being that keeps order to the universe. I have to say, though, that the idea that the world came to be as a result of a big bang is about as retarded an idea as I've ever heard."

"Have you ever read the *Tibetan Book of the Dead* or the *Kabbalah*?" she asked as she pulled her hair away from her face. "Now, I wouldn't try to tell you that any book is the absolute right answer, but I think we should glean the truths from all of these writings and form our own opinion. You said you believe in God. What does God represent to you?"

"Well, he is the one who created the universe. He is totally good and wants us to be totally good. That's why he gave us the Ten Commandments. He sent Jesus down here to die for our sins."

"Now, see," she said with a very serious look. She seemed like she was getting pretty jazzed up. "If God is so good and loving why did *he* let his own son die? Why does *he* let disease and hunger continue when people are suffering? There are babies that have cancer. Why does *he* let that happen? If we are *his* children and *he* wants us to be happy, why didn't *he* just stomp the breath out of Satan, spank Adam and Eve on the ass and tell them to behave, and let us live in the garden and run around naked and stuff? The reason the God you're referring to gave us the Ten Commandments was to keep us stressed out. No one can go through their entire life and not break at least half of the Ten Commandments."

Good God O'Mighty! The little old church ladies back home

would faint and fall over to hear her talk like that.

"So, you're telling me that God is a bad thing?"

"The story about God is good, and years ago it had a practicality. The human race used to need to feel that the great Father is watching them. If they were good, he would let them into heaven whenever they died. If they screwed up," she said in mock seriousness, "he would throw a lightening bolt at them and they'd be thrown into everlasting fire." She giggled. "But, come on. You know? This is 1973. Those stories were great for an ancient, unenlightened people, but we have to take responsibility for our own actions and face the consequences, whatever they may be."

"Well, I agree with that. However, I still believe that there is a supreme being to whom we will have to answer when we die."

"I'm not saying there isn't. I'm saying that the old picture of God, the old man with a long white beard sitting on a throne up there in the clouds being waited on hand and foot by angels, is archaic. God wants us to be happy, just the way we were in the garden." She paused for a minute. "Man, we really got deep, didn't we? I didn't mean to get so theological on you."

"No, that's cool. I don't have many friends that *can* be that deep. Most of the conversations we have go like, 'What do you want to do?' 'I don't know what do you want to do?' And so on until we just decide to go out and smoke some grass and come back in and listen to the Stones or Pink Floyd or whoever."

"I use drugs only ceremonially. Otherwise it really disrupts my karma."

"Oh, I don't hardly ever do that kind of stuff myself."

"Hey, if that's what you like to do, that's fine. Do it as long as you don't hurt anyone else. Personally, I like to stay in tune with the cosmos. That's the way the goddess wants us to be, anyway. She doesn't have a book full of don't-do's. She has a book that, in a nut shell, says, 'if it feels good, do it'."

"I've never heard of this book. What is it?"

"I'll show it to you when you're ready," she said as she scooted over closer to me. I put my arm around her, and we sat there looking at the waves rolling in and the mist that it created. I looked down at her and her bra was gapped open. Her nipple was in clear view and my eyes were locked on. I was enjoying the view when she said, "You know what, Ricky?"

"What's that?"

"When you were sitting across from me just now, your thingy was poking out of your pant leg."

How embarrassing.

Around eleven we packed up everything and drove east on the island until we were at all those little shops along the sea wall. We were walking hand in hand, and I was rather proud of myself. Things were going well.

As we were walking along the seawall she suddenly stopped and said, "You asked me what I do with my witchcraft. Do you still want to know?"

I was surprised. "Sure," I answered.

"You see that little old man across the street?" she asked.

There on the other side of the street was a homeless old man pushing a grocery cart full of all of his cherished possessions. To any other person it would have only been a load of junk. I'm sure to him it was his entire world.

"Yes, I see him," I answered.

"Watch," she said. She closed her eyes and tilted her head back slightly. Then she opened her eyes and watched for the result of her prayer.

A second later the old man bent down and picked something up off of the ground. It looked like an ordinary piece of paper. He gazed at it in unbelief, and then his jaw dropped as he examined it even closer. He looked around as he stuck it in his pocket, and then he shuffled quickly away.

"OK, what was all that about?" I asked.

"I gave him a twenty dollar bill," she beamed.

"You wished him to find the money? That's what you do with your witchcraft?"

"I wished the money there and for him to find it. I could have just as easily wished him to step into the street and get hit by a bus."

"How can you do that? Are you telling me these things happen just because you wish them to?" I asked her. I still didn't know whether or not to believe in this whole witchcraft thing.

"This is what I'm talking about. You would be a natural at this. I can teach you everything I learned in New Orleans. Wouldn't you like to have the kind of power I just showed you?" she asked, clinging to my shirt sleeve.

"Let me think about it," I said. "I'm interested, no doubt about that."

"Take whatever time you think you need, but remember, I won't be giving you this chance again. I know the time is coming when the world will see the power I possess. There is a spiritual revolution coming, and it's coming soon. It will be a battle of the forces of the Mother Goddess, Göndul, against those of the conventional church…the forces of good against the forces of evil. The evil forces want to suppress your spirit and make you live in the bondage of *don't-do-this* and *don't-do-that*. You want to be on the winning side, don't you?" she asked, looking at me as if to say that I would be a jackass to refuse her proposal. I almost felt like a jackass for the doubt that was going through my mind at the time.

"Yeah, sure!" I finally announced.

"That's why I'm giving you this chance to join with us. With me as the High Priestess and you, eventually, as the High Priest, you'll have power, popularity, anything you want. I cannot emphasize enough that last part. If you want *anything at all*, it will be supplied to you."

I was overwhelmed. I had only just met her, and she seemed to know all the thoughts and longings I had been having for all these years. As I stood there on the Galveston seawall with the cool winter wind blowing through my hair, the warm sun beating down on my face, and the sound of seagulls, waves, and cars all around me, the thought flashed through my mind that this could possibly be the girl for whom I was put on Earth for. I had heard the cliché of someone being another's soul mate, but I was beginning to think it might be true. It just seemed that everything was moving way too fast.

At three o'clock she said she was tired and felt like going home. We headed back for Humble and arrived at her house around five-thirty. Again, I didn't get out of the car.

"Well, I guess I'll probably talk to you tomorrow," I said.

She leaned over and kissed me a deep, wet kiss. That did it. My heart was now hers to do with as she pleased.

"We'll talk some more about what we talked about today," she said.

"OK. I'll call you. Are y'all listed in the book?"

"Oh, we don't have a telephone. Just come over about two tomorrow. Is that good?" she said tossing her bag over her shoulder.

"Yeah! I'll see ya about two."

No phone? I thought. *I thought everybody in the world had a phone.*

She walked to the house in the fading light of the evening, turned, and waved before going in. She also looked up at the sky again before she went in. I poked my head out to see what she was looking at. There was nothing there except a few early evening stars. I put the car in reverse and turned to begin to back out and there was my old buddy again—the dog. He was standing there behind me in the driveway just staring at me. He got out of the way when I began to back out, and when I got to the end of the long driveway I stopped the car for a minute and looked back up the drive toward the house. In absolute silence, with dust flying behind him as he ran and with the look as if a demon was forcing the canine teeth to grow larger, the dog was running full stride at me with wide wild eyes and jumped up on the hood of my Bug, looking directly at me through the windshield. His teeth had become long, white, and nasty. Saliva seeped onto the hood of my car from the corners of his mouth, which was snarled resembling a very evil looking smile. The hair on his back was spiked up indicating the rage welling up and spilling over through the foaming saliva. I popped the clutch with the car still in reverse and whipped out into the road quick enough to sling the mutt off the hood.

He rolled off into the road, and as I drove off that's where I last saw him, standing in the road, watching me.

When I got to the house I didn't feel like doing anything. I was spent—totally drained. I took a hot shower, went to my room, took off my robe, and lay down listening to the radio. It didn't take me long to fall asleep, even though the dog thing rattled me pretty badly. I thought maybe it was because of the dog I had the dream that night.

It was weird. I dreamed I woke up. I don't think I ever dreamed I woke up before. But, I woke up and got out of bed, naked, which is the way I went to bed. I would have normally put something on right away, but I didn't. I stood in front of my open bedroom window noticing how incredibly dark it was outside. There's a streetlight just outside that always shines in my window, but it was out, and there was no moonlight that I could see. As I stood there wondering about all these things, a cat jumped up onto my windowsill and came into the room. It was an average sized, silver furred cat.

"Well, come on in. I guess you'd be the first pussy I've ever had in this room," I chuckled.

The cat stood at my feet and I squatted down to stroke it. When I did, the cat changed from the cat that came in through the window, to Sylvia. Then to a form between Sylvia and Sylvia with cat-like features.

It seemed like one of those crazy little dreams I have as I'm going to sleep thinking about something serious when these stupid nonsense things pop into my head. Then about the time I realize I'm dreaming—CONK!—I'm asleep. But, I wasn't conking out in this one. Sylvia was speaking to me, but what I was hearing wasn't matching the movements of her mouth. It was like a movie with the audio out of sync. She was saying she could make me the High Priest of the church. I would hold all the power. She was the next in line as the High Priestess in North America, and she was going to teach me the incantations and ceremonies. I would be brought into their coven and share in the fruits of the work they are putting in when the revolution is a success, if I would only follow her directions.

"The night of your initiation is approaching," she said in a screechy animal-like voice. "It will be a night of feasting and merriment. Don't you want to come to the feast and enjoy more of this?" When she had finished speaking, she stood naked before me and seduced me, terribly and wonderfully, three times. After the third time I begged her to stop because of the energy that I had exhausted. She did stop after I had begged her for mercy. However, the entire dream repeated two more times after that.

CHAPTER 4

L ate Sunday morning I arose to an enchanting wake-up call. It was the lilting voice of my mother saying:"Are you going to sleep all day? Is this all you're ever going to do with your life? Get your butt outta that bed and get outside! I guess you think you're gonna be young forever, right? You're gonna wish you hadn't slept your youth away! If I only had a nickel for every time I wished I were young again, we would all have a very merry Christmas, thank you very much. Now, get up! Your father wants you to mow this yard before you go anywhere. You look like hell! Did you get drunk last night? If you get caught and thrown in jail, don't come crying to me to bail you out."

At that point I just left her talking. She probably went on with it for five minutes or so after I left. I've seen it happen with Dad before. She'll get on his case 'til she drives him out of the house, and then she'll talk to herself as if he's still there.

The grass was about ankle high when I pushed the mower out, so I fired it up and forty-five minutes later I was a free man. But, it was only 12:30, so I went and cruised Main Street. Main Street in Humble on a Sunday morning was pretty boring. All the church people were already down the road at the Log Cabin Restaurant and that pretty much just left me. I parked in front of the building that used to be the fire station in years past. In front of this building is a live oak spreading over two benches, which were the locally famous "wisdom benches" under the "tree of knowledge". The old guys sit here in the evening and talk about their glory days of playing football for dear old Humble High School.

I took a seat, lit one up and thought about last night. What a weird dream. That's all it was, after all, but what if it could be true. The part about having the power was kind of a turn on. I could tell this whole town to shove it, including the prom queen, the surfers, the kickers, and the football captain—Mr. Big Shot. Even the "I-crap-gold-turds-that-don't-stink-because-I-go-to-church-so-I'm-holier-than-thou" crowd would have to respect me or pay the price. I could have anything I want. I wonder if she meant *anything*. That old beat up VW could use some fixing up. To hell with that, I needed a new car. Maybe even a VW micro-bus. I'd get an apartment and a maid to keep it clean. And, I wouldn't need school anymore. I could go on vacations! Hell, I've never been *anywhere* except to Galveston! It would be so cool! I could finally go to Disneyland.

Yeah, like it's gonna happen. I came back to the real world where I am just a kid in a little town. I flipped the cig away and far up the street I saw a car. The first one I had seen since I got here. I watched it to see if it was someone I knew, but long before it got to me, it turned down another street. I took off to Sylvia's house. All this excitement was just overwhelming.

When I pulled into the driveway I started looking for the hellhound. He was nowhere in sight and I didn't know if that was a good thing or a bad thing. I parked it and sat there a few seconds. Maybe he was waiting over there, in the bushes, waiting for me to get between the car and the house. Then he would jump out and tear my arm off. Man! Was that paranoia talking or what? I gathered up my masculinity and got out of the car. No dog. I began to walk to the house. At the halfway point I looked around. Still…no dog. I was almost to the steps to the door when *he* crawled out from under the front porch—wagging his tail so hard his whole body was shaking and a long floppy tongue hanging out. It was like he wanted to say, "Where the heck have you been, old buddy? I have missed you like you wouldn't believe!"

Sylvia opened the door at about the same time. "Well, I see you've met Horus," she said as she descended the steps of the house. She took him by the head scratching behind his ears and started talking that doggy, baby talk, "He's a good boy. Yes, he is. He's Sylvia's baby, aren't you? Yes, you are."

"Oh, yeah. We're old friends. We go way back to night before last," I said as I patted him on the head. I half way expected him to take my hand off when I reached down to him, but he just stood there looking like, "Oh, yeah, man! Love me a lot. Scratch my back."

Sylvia invited me in, so in we went. Her mother was just inside the door, "Mother, this is Rick. Rick—my mother, Linda."

I shook her hand. I thought she was a young-looking mother, who was in her late thirties or so. She was dressed very old-fashioned, with a long black dress, and her hair was pulled up tight on her head into a bun. She asked, "Have you had lunch, Rick? I have some tuna salad made for sandwiches. That's Sylvia's favorite."

"Yes, ma'am. That would be fine," I replied.

Sylvia punched me in the ribs as her mother left the room. "Don't call her ma'am!"

I couldn't help but look at her in total disbelief—I mean this is southeast Texas. If you suspect a woman is ten minutes older than you are, you call her ma'am.

"She is my subordinate as well as my dad, Ogma, and I won't have them treated above their station," she said sternly. "In the church, I am royalty. You have to understand that and accept it."

Ogma? I thought. *What kind of name is Ogma?*

"She is in your church?" I asked her. "She's your subordinate? Well, what am I?"

"My entire family is in the church, and at the moment, you are my student. When you are accepted into the church you will be subject to me."

"It's odd you should say that because I had the weirdest dream last night and that was mentioned in it."

"Really? Isn't that strange?" she said in a tone of voice that was like, *So what?* "After we eat I will teach you two elementary spells," she said, changing the subject.

Her mother brought in the sandwiches along with chips and iced tea, put them down on the table, and I couldn't swear to it, but it looked like she sort of bowed. I mean, it was just a little one from the waist, but this was something new to me. I've never seen any kid get treated like this before—or since.

41

When we were through eating we went into the living room. It was a large room with old heavy French looking furniture and a smell of eucalyptus in the air. It was a smell that reminded me of my grandmother's house; it was dark and old. There was a china cabinet along the wall between the living room and the dining room and a coffee table in the middle of the room in front of the couch. There was no television, only an old hi-fi record player with a built in AM/FM radio. Doilies were on the arms of the chairs, and a large colorful Persian rug was in the middle of the wooden floor. The windows were darkened by heavy drapes that hung from just above the windows to the floor. The walls were decorated with a wallpaper design of small pink and white flowers on a blue background and the pictures that hung from the walls were mostly of flowers, also. There was one exception, however. There was a picture of a black woman on one wall, and underneath the picture was a table that had several candles on it of various colors. The picture had the name of the woman in the picture and it said *Marie Laveau.*

"The first thing I'm going to show you is actually a child's incantation, a birthday wish."

"You mean like make a wish and blow out the candles? I already know how to do that one," I said as I bit into my tuna sandwich.

"That's the customary way of doing it, but it's not the right way," she said as she took as sip of her tea. She continued on saying, "First, we take a little piece of paper and write a wish on it. Think of something you want and write it on here," she said, handing me a piece of paper and a little pencil.

I wrote my wish down on the paper.

"Now, fold it and hold it between your palms and think about what you wished for. Visualize it in your head. When you're finished go place your wish under that flower pot on the window sill behind the curtain, over there."

I did what she told me to do. I came back to the coffee table and finished my lunch.

"Soon that wish will come true, if you believe it will. Now, I'll show you a real incantation. First, we're going to do the candle ceremony."

She walked over to the hi-fi and put on a record. She said it wasn't essential for the spell we were about to do, but she liked the mood it set. It was Mozart's *Requiem—The Mass for the Dead*, and I have to admit, it wasn't bad. She went to the corner of the room and opened a wooden box, which had quite a few candles of all different colors. We sat down on the floor with our knees under us and our toes pointed down on the floor, much the same way people would kneel in front of a priest.

"What day were you born?" she asked.

"I was born on December 17th. I'm a Sagittarius, if that's what you want to know."

"This is the candle for Sagittarius," she said, taking out a purplish-blue candle and giving it to me to hold.

She took a white cloth out of the china cabinet drawer and spread it over the coffee table. Then she pointed her finger and made a circle around the table with us inside. Then waved her finger up, down to the left, across to the right, back up to the northwest side of her circle, and then down to the bottom. Then she placed four white tapered candles at each corner.

"These are the altar candles. They are always placed on each corner of the altar. Anything can be the altar, it just depends on where you are and what you have. Today, the coffee table will be our altar."

She got up and lit some strawberry incense and put one on each side of the room. Then she came back and sat down on the floor again.

"This yellow candle," she said, picking the candle up out of the box, "is for today, Sunday. The spell will be for your spiritual cleansing. You just meditate on that. Now, as we both hold the candle we bless it." She extended the bottom end of the candle to me and instructed, "Repeat after me, *On this holy day and for my spiritual need, I bless this candle.*"

I followed her lead. Each thing she told me to say, I said it.

She pulled another candle from the box and said, "Good, now, this is the Astral candle that coincides with you birthday as you've already seen. This is your candle. Now, we'll do the same with it."

She held it at one end, and I held it at the other as we chanted. *"On this holy day and for my spiritual need, I bless this candle."*

Pulling another candle from the box she continued, "This is the Offertory candle," she said, holding up a white candle. "This candle is for your spiritual enlightenment, cleansing and healing."

Again, she held it at one end and I held it at the other as we chanted. *"On this holy day and for my spiritual need, I bless this candle."*

When she had identified all the candles and carefully laid them out on the alter we picked up each candle again, and with a soft cloth and olive oil we lightly buffed each candle one at a time while she was chanting a little song whose words I did not know. We took turns buffing each of the candles. While buffing each candle we said, "My wax helper, I purge you of all negative energy. Be pure, fresh, and clean as a newly born soul." After we had said that, we both turned each candle over and, using a rose thorn, we scratched a star into the bottom, which was followed by another chant. "I hereby hallow you, my wax helper. May you always house the characteristics with which I am about to instill within you, and may you work in my service toward the goal of this sacred spell."

Before taking the Offertory candle she burned a bit of some sort of grass that was bound with red string. When the fire died down she moved the smoking bundle between her and me and then she said, "We will now rub the candle with a blessed oil to prepare it to work the spell. The blessed oil we will be using is Frankincense. We use different oils for different spells. This one is used for spiritual awakening. This is how we dress it. We are trying to get something, so we rub the candle down with the oil starting from the bottom, rubbing it all around until we get to the middle. Then we rub it from the top to the middle. If we were trying to cast something away we would do it the opposite way—from the middle to the bottom and then from the middle to the top."

When we got through dressing the candle she lit the altar candles with a wooden match. Then she took one of the altar candles and lit the day candle, the astral candle and then the Offertory candle, all three of which sat on the right front of the altar. When the candles were lit, she took two black scarves out of the box, and we put them over our heads. After that, she took out a knife she called an athame, a ritual dagger, and cut a small bit of hair from the back of my head. She tied the hair onto my candle with a cotton thread, and then placed the candle and the athame on the table. Her mother then brought in two little silver cups of wine, a small bowl of water, and another of salt. Sylvia took a pinch of salt and sprinkled it into the water and explained that it represented life. She took some of the brine water and touched it to her forehead, and then did the same to me.

As we held the wine cups up over the altar, as she instructed me to do, she called for a blessing on them, "Lady Göndul, Valkerie Warrior, bless the blood of the grape held here in your chalice. So may it be."

We placed the wine again on the table. Then, taking the athame, she pricked her finger and let three drops of her blood drip into my cup. Then she took my finger and stabbed it and let three drops fall into her cup.

"Mother of Werewolves, most beautiful of all angelic beings, take now as your servant, Richard Stevens, who will serve you by my side. He comes to you of his own free will and pledges his loyalty to the Temple of Göndul. Add his name to your book of life as he drinks the cup of blessing. So may it be."

We drank the bloody wine and that is the way it started.

"You are now dedicated to join the Temple of Göndul," she said, and then she took my scarf from my head and kissed me deeply and passionately.

"Go get the birthday wish from under that flower pot," I told her, which she did. She unfolded it and found the words, *I wish Sylvia would kiss me before I leave this house.*

"See?" she said. "It works."

"What's next?" I asked her. "When does the church meet?"

"That will be next Saturday, but before you are allowed to go in, you will have to go through a purification ritual. What we did here was just a dedication. You will come here after school every day next week and go to the tent that is being set up outside. In the tent is a book I will leave for you to study. There will be things explained in there for you, such as what the initiation ceremony will include. During that ceremony and the ceremonies to follow, you will do exactly what I tell you to do without hesitation. Can you do that?"

"Sure, I can do it," I said.

"Good. You answered quickly. I don't believe you will have any problems. You will study until nine o'clock each night. We will bring you some food. It won't be much, though. You will be on a fast."

"Sylvia, I love you with my whole heart, and I'll do anything for you, but my mom will have a cow if I'm not home at a decent time."

"I'll talk to her," she said.

"You don't know my mother. She is a little hard to talk to. Are you sure you want to do that?" I asked, trying to warn her.

"She won't have a problem with it. I promise," she said with a smiling face framed by her glorious brown hair.

"OK, but you realize, I told you I'd think about joining. I never told you I decided to join."

"Rick, when you were out this morning thinking about all the power you could have and what you could do with power like that, didn't you decide then that you were going to join?"

"How did you know about that?" I said as we got up and put all the ceremonial goodies away.

"I told you. I'm one of the most—if not THE most powerful witch in North America. That wasn't just a dream you had last night, either. I used shape shifting and astral projection to come into your dream, if that's what you want to call it. I was prepared to come back every night and screw you 'til your knees knocked to get you to join. I was right in seeing your enlightened state—the arts, literature, and a higher level of thinking. You're even left handed. Do you know what that is called?" she asked as we moved through the hallway stopping in front of a door. "It's called being sinistral. Right-handers are dextral and lefties are sinistral, the same word we get sinister from. I have great things planned for you and me. All these things are new to you, but soon you will see what a life changing effect it has on you. The tent is ready, so now you must go into the tent and die."

"What do you mean die?" I asked obviously confused.

"In any religious initiation ceremony the inductee goes through a period of transformation—from a former way of life into the new life. Between the two he passes through death, symbolically speaking. While you are in the tent studying, you are in death. You won't see your friends or family, and then on the night of the induction ceremony you will be reborn into the new life. You need to start now. The tent is ready."

She opened the front door, and there was a rather large canvas tent. I'm sure it wasn't there when I drove up.

A black gentleman was there finishing up with the tent. He appeared to be about fifty years old or so, bald on top of his head, and he was very friendly.

"Rick, this is Jimmy Williamson. He takes care of the lawn and building maintenance for Ogma. Jimmy, this is Ricky."

"I'm very happy to meet you, Rick. I hope you'll be comfortable in the temporary quarters. If there is anything I can get you to make it a little more bearable, you don't hesitate to contact me. OK?" he said as he shook my hand.

"Sure, thanks, Jimmy. I'm sure it will be great."

Now, that I didn't have to worry about Horus gnawing my leg off, I had a chance to look around at the layout of the property.

On the right of the driveway, close to where my car was parked and well out of view of the road, there was a clothesline suspended by two cast iron poles that had, at one time, been painted silver. Now, they were pocked with rust spots where the paint had peeled away. Along the clothesline there were four large, menacing looking, hooks. I was puzzled about what that was. The house, a large white wooden house, was on the west side of the property. On the north side of the property was a big barn facing south. It was one of the biggest barns around Humble, at least as far as I had seen. On the right side of the barn was a travel trailer—one of those Silver Stream trailers. It had electricity hooked up to it and looked like someone was staying in it.

"Is there someone living in the trailer?" I asked Sylvia as we walked out to the tent.

"It is our family's custom for the men and the women to sleep in separate buildings. Bruce and Ogma sleep out there."

It seemed to me what she said was a little sick and unnatural. There were a lot of things about this family that I was beginning to realize I would be surprised about.

"I'm sorry, that was none of my business. I shouldn't have pried," I apologized.

"It's OK. I'm not ashamed of it. It is a healthy thing for people to remain celibate as long as possible and to concentrate on the things the god and goddess are wanting. Nighttime is good for prayer and meditation."

We came to the tent entrance.

"So, here is your new home," she said as we stood in front of the tent.

We went inside the green canvass structure where there had been set up a comfortable looking easy chair, a reading lamp, a large tub of water, a table with some towels on it, and beside the chair, a small table with a book on it. *A Book of Guidance for the Traveler— Becoming a Witch* was on the cover along with a star inside of a circle.

"This is like an elementary reader," Sylvia said, picking up the book, and then setting it down again. She began to walk slowly around the tent. "It's just something to get you started. Everything you need to get you through the initiation is in there. When you come in here the first thing you need to do is take off all your clothes and jewelry and bathe," she said, pointing to the tub. "No one will disturb you, and there will be fresh wash cloths and towels every day. Then you can put your clothes back on and begin to study. I will come in once a day and bring you your food, which will be bread, honey, and milk. That is all you will eat every day. You need to take that for your lunch at school, too. I will also bring you one of these every day." At that point she gave me another one of those long kisses that made things pretty hard, if you get my drift, and she knew it.

As she turned to leave she said, "Oh, yes. You will also remain celibate."

Well, I thought, *I've had eighteen years of practice at that. It shouldn't be too hard.*

48

CHAPTER 5

The next five days went by in a blur. I went to school then I went to Sylvia's house, went straight to the tent, stripped, washed, redressed, and studied. At first the bread and honey thing was pretty crappy, but after a couple of days it got better. Maybe it was because I was starving, and I could have eaten a tennis shoe and it would have been delicious. I believe the fasting was good for me spiritually, and I think it also helped me to think clearer. And the affection I got from Sylvia was intensifying. The kisses were getting longer and longer, and my natural instinct was getting more aroused each time. My balls ached from the arousal. On Friday evening she finished her kiss and I told her how I wanted her. While I held her in my arms I pledged my undying love to her that was certain to endure through eternity.

"Sylvia, I love you like I have never loved anyone ever in my entire life. I have had crushes on girls before. I've even experienced puppy love, but this is different. I can feel this with the essence of my soul. My heart is about to pop with the love it holds for you."

"Ricky, you are the one I want to be in my life for many years to come. I knew that you were special the day I laid eyes on you. I care for you, too. But right now you have to study for the initiation. After that we can think about the future. Tonight you are entering into the last twenty-four hours. It is critical to remain pure." She kissed me again. "OK?"

"Yeah, I can do it," I told her as she left the tent.

I had learned a lot from the book. I was ready.

I went into the tent at 4:00 p.m. on Saturday evening. I would be initiated on the new moon during the festival of Imbolic before the entire coven. I had met no one in the coven as of yet, except for Sylvia and her mother. I had studied the book, front and back, and could answer all of the questions that were going to be asked of me. The one thing I had practiced intently all week was to show no emotion. On that subject, I found a small book on the life and philosophy of the Stoics in the school library. It wasn't much, but it served to help me learn to accept things as they are presented to me. Once it is spoken or done, it is done. There is no need to be surprised or show expressions. I didn't believe there was anything that would be done to cause me to draw from the Stoics, but Sylvia pointed out several times not to show emotion during the rite.

The sun was about to set and I was ready. It was again a warm night. For it to be a warm night in February was very unusual, but it was good, as I would be skyclad throughout the majority of the ceremony, which was being held in the barn. At least I would have some protection from the coldness. Not much, but some. I took the purification bath in a warm tub of salt water. After I bathed I donned an old, moth-eaten robe that Sylvia brought to me to wear from the tent to the barn.

The time came and two people in hoods, a male and a female (the maid and the squire for my initiation) beckoned me to follow, and we walked the twenty yards or so to the barn. Through the barn doors we came into an entry hall—a small room before the main hall—the anteroom before entering the temple. It was a dark room painted black on all of the walls with no furnishings or adornment except for a small table with a bowl and a solitary candle on it. In this anteroom, I removed my robe and stood naked to be anointed. My heart was racing as I did this because it was the first time I had ever been naked in front of people that I didn't know. The squire anointed me first. Using brine water from the bowl, he made the mark of the Celtic cross on my forehead—a circle with a cross in it. After he did that, he took some more water and made the pentagram on my left breast, over my heart. The maid then dipped her hand into the water and made an inverted triangle from my genitals, to my right breast, to my left breast and back to my genitals. I was now anointed to enter the temple, but at this point I was still not allowed entrance.

The initiation started with the maid and squire stepping through the door into the temple. The squire stated that a traveler had come from a long way seeking the things this group enjoyed.

The priest asked, "Who can vouch for this person?"

"I can," Sylvia declared, "as his teacher I have shown him the way, pointed him in the right direction, and set his feet on the right path. But he has chosen to take this step and now bids you give him entrance."

The maid and squire came back to where I was in the anteroom. The maid put a blindfold over my eyes and the squire bound my arms behind me looping it around my neck, all with the same cord. At this point I was at their mercy. I was naked, blind folded, and tied up.

They led me into the temple and the ceremony began. I answered the questions as they were put to me. They were mostly to affirm that I had come on my own free will seeking the joy and fellowship of the coven. They rang the ceremonial bell and finally the priest ordered me to face those whom I sought. At that point they removed the blindfold and I could see the inside of the temple for the first time. The barn had been transformed into a gothic cathedral illuminated with torches and draped with black curtains. Decorative gargoyles were painted gold and held the torches, and at the back of the temple was a huge painting of a white goat's head. The head was flanked on each side by a huge red velvet curtain that was tied back revealing the head. The goat's head was painted with three numbers on the forehead, 666, in red paint. On the floor where the priest stood was a large white pentagram with an altar in the center of it. Around me were all the members of the coven, robed and bear headed. There were about twenty people that made up the coven, and many of those people I had never met before. However, there were several people there I knew from school. Many of them were girls I had always wanted to date, but the crowd they associated with never accepted me. That crowd that they associated with was here. It was apparently a major portion of the coven. I tried to hide my nervousness of standing there nude in front of all these people. When I realized they had all gone through the same humbling experience I was now going through it helped me to relax, but only a little.

While I was away in la-la land, the ceremony had been continuing. I snapped out of it when there were two ceremonial daggers in front of my eyes being held by Sylvia and her father, who was acting as the temple's Priest. I had almost missed my cue.

I kissed each athame and said, "I salute the Lord and Lady, as I salute those who represent them. I pledge my love and support to them and to my brothers and sisters of the Craft."

"Know you the dictum of Wicca?" the priest asked.

"I do," I answered and quoted the Wiccan motto, "Yea, if it harms no one, do what you will."

"And do you abide by that rede?" he asked.

"I do."

The priest then asked, "What say you of yourself to the God and Goddess to whom you pledge?"

I answered, "I embark upon this path of my own free will and for the good of myself and of the coven to which I am bound. I will follow the Wiccan motto...Yea, if it harms no one, do what you will. I do not seek power over others for vengeance sake, but aim to increase my own knowledge, self esteem, and happiness through the Craft. I claim and hold to the law of manifold return: What I cast into the elements of earth, wind, fire, water, and sky will return to me three times more powerful. I promise to keep the identity of my brothers and sisters secret and help protect them from harm. I shall follow my coven's rulings as handed down by the Goddess's handmaiden, her High Priestess, and the laws set forth to the best of my ability. I will continually strive to gain a truer and deeper understanding of the Craft. I will respect all life as sacred and treat the earth and its worthy inhabitants with love and compassion. I thank the God and the Goddess for this path on which my feet have been set, and I promise to uphold the best traditions of the Craft.

"Well said. Let your bonds now be loosed that you may be reborn," the High Priest declared.

They untied me, and it felt good to have the cord taken from around my neck. My hands went cold as the blood flowed back into them.

The priest announced to the members present that since I am starting a new life I would have a new name of my own choosing.

"Have you chosen that name?" he asked.

"I have."

"Declare the name that you have chosen."

"It is Drahcir."

"Then from this place forward you shall be Drahcir called by your brothers and sisters in the Craft."

The High Priestess, Sylvia, whose witch name was Tara, then anointed me with oil going over the places I was first anointed to enter the temple—the cross, the pentagram, and the triangle.

As she anointed me with the oil she prayed, "O, Göndul, Great Valkyrie Warrior, bight lady of the awakening soul, accept Drahcir as your servant. Drahcir, with this sacred oil I anoint and cleanse thee, giving new life to you…a child of the gods," she said. "From this day forth you shall be known as Drahcir, within this circle and without it, to all of your brothers and sisters of the Craft. So may it be."

When she was finished anointing me with oil, I was brought a new robe to wear and I placed the old robe into the ceremonial fire, symbolically consuming my former life in tongues of flame.

After a few more proclamations and bell ringings, the ceremony concluded by the priest announcing, "Now you are truly a member of the Temple of Göndul. As one of us, you will share in our knowledge of the gods and of the art of healing, of divination, of magick, and of all the mystic arts. These you shall learn as you progress."

"But we caution you," the High Priestess added, "ever to remember the dictum of Wicca: Yea, if it harms no one, do what you will."

At this point the entire coven echoed the rule, "Yea, if it harms no one, do what you will."

"If it harms no one," the priest concluded, "do what you will. Come now, Drahcir, and meet your kindred."

I was led around the circle and was introduced to all the members, my new brothers and sisters. Then the priest rang the bell the final three times.

"Now it is truly a time for merrymaking," he said.

After the ceremony, the temple was cleared of the ceremonial furnishings. Food was brought out around the outer parameter of the circle. Wine was poured and pipes of marijuana was smoked. It was turning into the best party I had ever been to. Everybody ate until they were full and the weed and wine seemed to be endless. We partied well into the night.

Tara's brother walked over with a couple of my new siblings and introduced himself, "I am Tara's brother, Judex," he said, handing me a glass of wine. "Welcome to the family. I would like to toast you, if you don't mind."

He gave me no time to answer, but raising his voice above the din of the crowd and his glass high in the air he announced, "Here is to our newest brother, Drahcir, who has traveled for eighteen years to find us. May he find joy, rest, and love in this family."

I hoisted my glass with all the rest and emptied it in one swallow. I was already getting pretty hammered, and the party was showing no signs of slowing down. Tara was at my side and I felt great. Some of the girls, who before would have never even looked at me, were actually crowding around me to talk. I entertained the thought that during the ceremony they may have seen a side of me they hadn't seen before and it caught their interest.

I talked to a lot of people including Tara's father, Ogma. He told me that now that I am included in the circle I should address him by his witch name, Osix. I guess anything was better than Ogma. He seemed to be a very pleasant person. He was far more in tune with the attitudes of the young people of the day. He was not like the other adults I had known growing up. Tara's mom (witch name: Isadora) was not as out going as her husband, but she was a pleasant person to talk to. I really hit it off well with her brother, Bruce, aka Judex. He was going to help me with my studying. I was really kind of surprised he was so friendly. He was older than me by a couple of years.

As my wine glass got empty, someone filled it. The brothers and sisters gathered around and soon everyone was huddled around me.

Tara held her hand up and everyone got quiet. I was pretty drunk, and the sudden hush took me off guard. I giggled.

"Brothers, the time had arrived to seal the journey of the traveler, our brother, Drahcir," she said.

Judex caught me under the arms and another guy grabbed my ankles. They laid me down on the floor and removed my robe. I was struggling until Tara whispered in my ear not to struggle; it was part of the acceptance into the coven.

"They're going to put the mark of the coven on you," she said in my ear. "Don't be mad. They do it because they accept you. I have the mark, too. See?"

She pulled her robe up revealing her closely trimmed little coochie. Just above it, on her left pelvis, was a yellowish-green crescent moon. It wasn't very big, about the size of a quarter, but it was very detailed. It had the face of the man-in-the-moon like all of those little cartoon pictures of the man-in-the-moon. It was kind of pretty.

"Now, hold still while they shave you," she told me. O-o-o I didn't like the sound of that.

Someone had a wet washrag scrubbing my pubic hair in the same area as Tara's. It took a while, and believe me, I held very still as they shaved my pubes. I didn't want them to slip while using that straight razor. Everyone was standing around watching, which was kind of annoying. I was in a very humiliating position here, and all these people were getting a real close look at my stuff. They started the tattooing, which hurt worse with every stick of that needle, but I figured if I weren't drunk it would hurt a helluva lot more than the piercing pain that I felt right now. It seemed like it took a long time, but what seemed to be an eternity finally ended. I was tattooed as were all the members of the coven. A cheer went up from the crowd as they declared the tattooing a success.

I was given my robe back and Judex handed me a mirror to check out my new art work. It was swollen with a lot of red streaks on the tattoo, and I thought that it didn't look very good.

"Don't worry, man. It'll take a day or so to look right, but it *will* look right. I do first rate ink," he grinned while taking a drink of wine.

The party went on long into the night; the night went on long into my life. It was the night on which I could look back and say this was the one that changed my karma. From that point forward I was accepted into a group at school that I had always wished I could be in. Not only was I accepted into the group, I soon was their leader. Being the teacher's pet had its perks.

CHAPTER 6

It seemed my parents were no longer concerned about me the way they had been. As soon as Tara told me she would talk to my parents, it was as if she had done it right then, and everything came out all right. I spent all the time I wanted to at the Chase's house studying, which went on way into the evening hours. Usually, it was Judex and Tara that instructed me, and other times it was just Judex. He never looked down on me. He just accepted me, and it really put me on the defensive. He was already going to college over in Baytown, and I was just a senior in high school.

About a week after my initiation he and I were going over some incantations when I finally got up the nerve to ask him, "Why do you treat me so nice?"

"I like you, man. You're a pretty cool dude."

"No, man, college guys don't hang out with high school guys. Don't get me wrong, I appreciate the help with the magic and spells, but why do you do it?"

"You're Tara's guy. You're the teacher's pet, you might say. She is grooming you for a High Priesthood, and she wants it done in a year. Normally it takes three years to become a third degree witch," he said, taking a drag from his cigarette. "But, if Tara wants it in a year, then Tara gets it in a year."

"And what is that all about? I have never seen any eighteen-year-old girl get treated like royalty like she does."

"What has she told you about herself?"

"She told me she's the most powerful witch around, and she has big plans for her and me."

Judex rubbed his chin in a thoughtful manner like he was trying to choose his words carefully. He walked to the corner of the room and turned to look back at me as he began to rub the back of his neck with a furrowed brow. From where I was sitting, this didn't look good.

"It sounds to me like you may not be aware of what you've gotten into. You certainly sound like you don't know who Tara is or what power she has. My sister," he continued as he took a final drag from his smoke and then crushed it out in the ashtray, "is the leader of this coven. There is no other coven for three miles in any direction. However, three miles in any direction from our boundary are other covens that have a priestess that presides over them. That priestess answers to my sister if there is a screw up or if there is a matter that takes an outside pair of eyes to judge. It goes on into district—the priestess of those covens in the district hold offices that regulate activities on the district level, and they report to my sister. And so it is on the regional and state level—just like in school competition. My sister sits as the head witch on the national level. She is like the witch president of the United States. Above her is the High Priestess of North America, then there is the High Priestess of the Western Hemisphere, and above her are the Illuminati. Those are the people that run the world."

"They run the world? I thought that was the job of the president of the United States, the Soviet Union, and England and all the other super-power nations of the world," I said as we stepped outside into the fresh winter air. We lit up another smoke and I said, "Aren't they the ones with their finger on the big red button?"

"Those guys don't make a move without talking to the Illuminati first."

"So who are the Illuminati?"

"They are made up of the High Priestess of Witches of Mother Earth and the head guy from the Warlocks of the World. Those two are of the Church of Witches and are appointed for life-time positions. There is one more person, and that person is the one who holds power over the other two and everyone else under them. I'm not allowed to name his name, all I can tell you is he has been in that position for a long, *long* time."

I don't know—was this guy just trying to scare me or what? He was doing a pretty fair job of it if he was.

"I'm not doubting what you're saying for a second, but if Tara has all of those responsibilities, why isn't she at some office somewhere in Washington. Doesn't she have meetings to attend?"

"Most of her big time meetings happen after the Yule festival in December. Any other meetings she, and all the rest who hold these meetings, uses astral projection to do business. They can go into a deep state of meditation and leave their body as a spirit to be somewhere else, or sometimes they will use it to catch someone else in a deep state of meditation and go in and put thoughts in their head. It's what they call seeding. There are times they will shape shift— assume the shape of an animal. Tara likes the form of a cat."

"Yes, I know," I told him. "She has been to see me in my dreams."

"She actually went inside your dream?" he looked stunned.

"Oh, yeah, she certainly did."

It looked like something I said actually surprised him. That was a switch. "Is that something you didn't know about?"

"I knew it was possible," he said, putting his cigarette out obviously a little rattled. "Tara and I had a little sibling competition going to see who would be able to do it first. I wonder why she didn't mention it."

"What about your mother and father?" I asked, "What about the disciplining and all the other parent stuff they're supposed to do?"

"When Tara went away to school in New Orleans she was six. Up until then my parents did all the disciplining. In New Orleans she was in a witch's school that was set up just like a Catholic school. The sisters would do any type of disciplining there was to do, and they were very strict. Tara was taught all the regular school stuff, along with black magic and voodoo. Through the years she elevated at such an unusual rate of speed the sisters called her the Daughter. It really started out as a joke, but after a while they stopped smiling when they called her that. She excelled in everything she did, graduating at the top of her class. She is at the college post-graduate level in the arts, math, and religious studies. She goes to your high school because she really just doesn't have anything else to do.

"You know, she calls this a Wiccan coven, but it is not Wiccan in the pure sense of the word. A Wiccan is one who practices white magic only, and that is to help people who are sick. They worship Mother Earth and are tolerant of all other religions who don't believe there is only one way. Tara mixes in black magic, voodoo, shamanism, and even a little of the Egyptian beliefs," he paused for a few seconds to light another cigarette. "How did you meet Tara, anyway?"

"I was sitting in band practice at school one day and looked up and there she was. I couldn't keep my eyes off of her. I thought about her all the next day, too. When I finally went up and introduced myself it was like we just clicked, like instant karma, you know?"

"Instantly clicked, huh?" he just stood there a few seconds looking at me. "Well, listen, if you two hit it off instantly, like you said, then I'm happy for you. She doesn't make mistakes. The sisters taught her to be absolutely sure about a decision when she makes one, so when she does she has thought it over for a long, long time. I have been helping you because she and I both see the potential in you to become a really good priest."

Walking into the room while Judex was in mid-sentence Tara sat down in the big armchair near the door. She acted as if she had not heard the discussion we had been having.

"So, what do you see in me? What attracted you to me, Tara?" I asked.

She smiled and averted her eyes from me for a couple of seconds. Sounding as if she were choosing her words carefully she said, "I see in you power and enlightenment." She rose again from the chair and walked over to me. "You are not like others around here who can barely see past Houston. You have a deep inner need of rising above the common people that you have been surrounded by for all these years. You've read great works, such as the classics and the little noted books as well, that make you feel free. That is because you can escape into them and be the hero on horse back on some snowy mountain, or the star-crossed lover who would give his own life for the woman he loves. You've read about people who have harnessed the great secrets you are now studying. You've tasted, only in your imagination, the energy they possessed. You have studied the musical arts by being taught how to play and appreciate the music you play on the trumpet. You have taught yourself how to play the guitar, the bass guitar, isn't it? You are even interested, in a secret way, in the oils and the watercolors of artists in that medium, isn't that true? I see in you a strong potential, but you lack the tenacity—the life force that it requires. Tonight we will perform a ritual to give you that life force. You will feel the power surge through you like you only imagined it would feel like, but you will feel it to an even greater degree."

"Yes," I agreed. "You are right about all these things you have said. I want to be a strong and powerful witch like you. I want to be successful. Show me what I have to do and I will do it."

"Tonight at midnight, during this full moon, we will offer a sacrifice to Damballah, the voodoo serpent-god, to give you a renewed life force. During that ritual you will be beside me and we will begin a new chapter in the life of this coven. It will be a small ceremony, but it will be the beginning of the overthrow of that which has kept the human race bound for all these centuries."

The evening came and it was time for the sacrifice. I had not studied about sacrificing anything, so it took me by surprise that we were, in fact, going to do it. I knew, however, that this was the path I wanted to take. In the few short days I had been in the church, I had already felt a sense of power and belonging that I had never felt before by hanging out with my other friends, like Don and Monkey and all the rest of that mediocre crowd. As Tara's chosen disciple, I was given preferential treatment by the people she called her underlings.

Those underlings began to arrive. The whole coven was not present. It was only those who were the special ones of her flock. These were her chosen ones. It was Tara's inner circle. There was me and Judex and his girlfriend, Chakkra. We were her *crem-de-la-crem*. The rest were made up of the clique I had always admired at school. The girls, by their witch names, were Astra, Luna, Owlen, and Aura. The guys were Styx, Sigurd, Raven, Bragi, and Bres, all of whom were high school class officers, counting Tara, thirteen in all.

We all, except Tara, met at the clothesline that was at the northeast end of the property. On the east side of the clothesline was an altar set up with the candles, athames, and oils for the ceremony. Within a few minutes of everyone's arrival, Tara came from the barn holding a lit ceremonial candle and wearing only a pentagram necklace. One at a time, we approached Tara, removed our robe, and were anointed with the oil the way I was anointed during my initiation. We were also given the prayer chants on a piece of paper. After Tara cast the circle the ceremony began. I stood at her side as she went through the ceremony that was clearly voodoo in nature. Soon she began to chant a prayer to Damballah, and we all answered at the appropriate places. As she offered up the prayer, Judex brought out a small dog that was tied by its feet, front and back, and hung it over one of the four large hooks along the clothesline. The little creature didn't struggle very hard, and I thought it might have been drugged. When she came to the end of her prayer she clasped the athame and punctured the dog in the neck. It was a very small hole, but it bled badly.

When the next part of the ceremony came I had doubts that I would be able to keep my promise about doing whatever it would take to achieve my goal. Tara caught some of the pouring blood into a goblet and held it out for me. I mustered my strength and showed no hesitation in taking the goblet from her. If I had, the brothers and sisters would have seen my weakness, and at this point I didn't know what would have happened. As the dog was in the process of dying a slow death, I drank the blood, passed the goblet to the next worshipper, and praised Damballah for the life force he had given me. I struggled to swallow the warm, thick liquid, but swallow it I did. When the last person had drank of the blood, the ceremony moved into the warmth of a small room in the back of the sanctuary where it turned into an orgy of sex and drugs, with no one showing any preference for whom they were with, male or female—except me. I was going to be with Tara, and I wouldn't let that change. The expression on the face of those copulating in the cool air was wild. Their features had changed into almost animalistic contortions. This was all going on as the dog drew its last breath hanging in helpless humiliation on the clothes line from a meat hook.

The following day Judex dug a shallow grave just outside of the area where the circle had been cast and buried the carcass.

CHAPTER 7

It was three in the morning when I got home. I sat in the car looking at the house. It was the same old house I had grown up in. The names of some of my old girlfriends were carved in some of the bricks. Out in the back yard was the oak tree I used to climb up in. I nailed a couple of boards up there about a decade ago, and that was the closest I ever came to having a tree house. The boards rotted away and are long gone now. On the east side of the house is where Sheryl and I buried some treasure. It was a little pill bottle Mom gave us that we filled it up with some fool's gold that we found in a pile of crushed marble. A neighbor who was remodeling his house was using the marble. We filled the bottle with the rocks and put a Troll doll in it and buried it, and then we forgot where exactly we buried it. We never found it again. I guess it might still be there to this day.

As I sat there with all of these memories going through my mind, I knew this was still the house my blood relatives lived in and where I could come and sleep, shower, and eat. But was it still my home?

I opened the front door as quietly as I could and found my way to my bedroom. I took off my watch and laid it on my desk. I stood there in front of the mirror for a while looking at myself. I had just turned eighteen a couple of months ago. Still a teenager—a kid. Most people my age were getting all jazzed up about going to college. Some were talking seriously about getting married, while others were going to join up for a hitch in the military, which didn't make any sense to me because Vietnam was starting to get pretty scary. Nixon came on the TV every other day and announced he was going to send over 30,000 more troops like it was just the thing to do. Bomb Cambodia? Why not? There were pictures of the war on the news every night, pictures that would later be considered too graphic for

TV. One report showed the execution of a known assassin. He was shot in the head right there on prime time TV. They also showed the picture of the little girl and her brother running naked and on fire, down a Vietnamese street after their village had been destroyed by napalm bombs, a gelatinous gasoline that was dropped in fifty-five gallon drums with a detonator attached. The little girl and her brother had the burning napalm covering a large part of their bodies. They ran nude and on fire down the street. The photographer won the Pulitzer for that. The evening news would give us the update on the day's battles. Every report was so lop-sided it was almost humorous to the average American. "The US forces killed 2,000 enemy troops while we lost only three US soldiers, two of the three were from heat exhaustion." The report was always like that, or at least something similar in stupidity, almost every day for years. I guess the government thought the population of the United States was made up of a bunch of dimwitted patriots that would believe such propaganda. The sad thing was that a lot Americans *did* believe such garbage.

If the news was not about the war in Vietnam, then it was on the riots in protest of the war in Vietnam or riots for racial equality. The blacks had a legitimate beef, the American Indians definitely had a good cause, and the Latinos didn't get vocal enough.

This was the kind of world I was living in. I am still a young man. Why do I feel so much older than I am?

I kicked off my boots to lie down on my bed, lit a cigarette, and thought about all the changes that had happened in my life. In a matter of weeks I had grown-up, or at least, that's the way it felt. Now it didn't matter when I got home. It didn't matter when I left. It didn't matter what I did. Mom and Dad let me come and go as I pleased and do whatever I wanted to do. It was the freedom I always wanted. It sucked. The people in this house didn't care about me anymore. About a year ago, if I had lit a cigarette here in my room, they would have run in and thrown a bucket of water on me, assuming that I must have been on fire because I knew they didn't allow smoking in the house. I really don't doubt that I could smoke weed in here and they wouldn't care.

"What are you doing?" I looked up and there was my little sister in the doorway.

Sheryl had her thick brown hair all down in her face, and the gown she was wearing looked like a big tow-sack on her little skinny frame with the head and arms cut out.

She came in and sat on the edge of the bed looking out of two sleepy slits for eyes. She had been asleep, but she said the front door opening woke her up. I handed the cigarette to her and she took a drag.

"Where have you been?" she asked, blowing out the smoke that she never inhaled. "It's three in the morning."

"I was just with some friends," I told her, taking the smoke back from her.

"Were you with Don? He's been looking for you. He said you've been acting weird at school and hanging around with a different crowd. Are you mad at him or something?" she asked, trying in vain to get her hair out of her face.

"I'm not mad at him. I just hang out with those other guys, now. They're gonna make something of themselves and not rot in this little town," I told her. "Why? Are you worried about me?"

"I'm worried about you and me and John, all three of us. Ever since that girl came over and talked to Mom about you, it's like Mom isn't like she used to be. She doesn't yell, she doesn't holler, she doesn't gripe to herself about anything...it's weird. Dad just goes with the flow. I liked it better when we knew what we could and couldn't get away with. Who was that girl, anyway?"

"That was my girlfriend, Sylvia. I've been seeing her for about a month now. Were you here when she talked to Mom?"

"Yeah. She's pretty. Why does she wear all black? Doesn't she like peace and flower power and all that stuff?" In Sheryl's room her walls were covered with big colorful flowers and pictures of her idols, Davy Jones, David Cassidy, Bobby Sherman, and Elvis Presley.

"She's not into that stuff, too much. She was brought up in New Orleans, and they don't have that, yet. I guess it's like it's filtering across from California and just hasn't reached there. Did you hear them talking?"

"No. I saw Mom get her and Sylvia a coke, and they sat at the dining room table and talked. They were laughing and everything. Now, there was one time when Mom went back to the kitchen for a minute, Sylvia stood up and waved a stick around Mom's chair. She waved it in a circle, and then she waved it from side to side, and then up and down while she whispered something. She sat down and had the little stick put away before Mom got back from the kitchen. What was that all about?"

"Sylvia has some strange ways, kiddo. You might not understand it if I told you."

"Does it have to do with witchcraft?"

I was shocked that she was so perceptive. How could she know about things like that?

"A few years ago, when I used to listen to my transistor radio late at night on KILT, right after the *Weird Beard* show they had the Alex Bennett talk show, and then after that was a show with a witch named Sybil Leek. Sometimes she talked about using one of those little sticks. It's a wand. Sybil Leek said she was a white witch. Is that what Sylvia is?" Sheryl asked me.

"If I said she was a witch, what would you think about that?"

"I think it would be cool. Are you learning witchcraft? Can you teach me? Is it hard?"

I looked at my little sister, now wide-eyed and beautiful, and thought about her innocence and naïvety. When she was a little girl she would catch frogs and kiss them to see if they would turn into a handsome prince. I would tease her and make her mad at me in the living room, then sit in a chair and let her try to beat me up, which only got me tickled and laughing at her. That would make her more mad and want to hit me more. Before her friend, Paula, moved in across the street she didn't have any little girl friends to play with, so I would play Barbie with her, as long as I could be Ken. When we went shopping I would pick out clothes for her so she could look hip. Looking back now, I guess she had always been my best friend. We didn't fuss and fight all the time, like other brothers and sisters. She was a good kid. I couldn't see her doing the same things I was doing. The Craft was a wonderful thing to me. I could handle the ugly side of it, which was done for the good of the final outcome, but Sheryl had never been exposed to anything as ugly as some of the ceremonies were. I loved her more then to get her involved in something like that.

"No, I don't know about the witchcraft thing. Maybe she was just doing a good luck thing around her chair or something."

Something over my bed suddenly came off the wall and hit me on the head. It had force behind it, and it hurt pretty badly.

"Oh, crap! Are you OK?" Sheryl asked, looking at my head. "That was weird! Perfect timing! That scared me half to death."

"I'm OK," I said, pulling away from her. I didn't let her know it had scared me too. I was sure it wasn't just coincidence. "I guess I better try to go to sleep now. I'll see ya tomorrow."

"OK, bubba. Night-night," she said as she left the room.

I turned off the lamp on my nightstand and laid there a few minutes thinking about what Sheryl had said. Tara had put a spell on Mom. I had been almost certain of that from the beginning, anyway. My mom certainly wouldn't put up with the way I had been acting under normal conditions. If she put a spell on Mom, what else might she have done?

I got up out of bed and found my altar in the dark. It wasn't much, just a little table close to the window where by day it was a place for my records to sit. In this situation, I could turn it into an altar. I went through all the formalities of erecting the temple, opening the circle, and lighting the candles. I brought out a crystal ball. One of my gifts, according to Tara, was scrying or fortune telling. She said that it was a gift. I just dabbled with it, but she said I was too good at it just to play with it. I could divine the past of those in the coven when they would tell me of a time in their lives. I could look back at that time and tell them if there were circumstances that they hadn't been aware of, or consequences of their actions that may still be forthcoming. I could also foretell the future, and I had used it for Astra one day about a week ago.

Astra was a very beautiful girl with blond hair, blue eyes, shapely figure, and a lot of charisma. She came to me one day and said she was going to put a love spell on one of the football jocks at school. She knew the spell was going to work, but she wondered if he would be everything she wanted him to be. I got everything going and gazed into the crystal. What I saw I didn't want to know about. The guy was the stuff, all right, as far as all the girls were concerned, and he was a rough, muscular guy. Unfortunately, he didn't care much for girls. He had a secret affair going on with one of the guys on the debate team. The debate team guy was very effeminate and spoke with a lisp, but until now I thought it was just a speech impediment. Astra was surprised, but she was going to cast the spell anyway. There was no competition from other girls, and she would take care of this other guy. If the kid gave up Mr. Football, good, if he didn't, Astra said her motto had always been, "Two is company and three's a party."

I was also able to see the present from a perspective that is not normally seen. I could see from every angle of the situation, the good and the bad. That is what I was doing tonight. I was going to divine the truth about Tara. I sat the crystal in the middle of the black velvet cloth I spread out on the altar. It was a beautiful ball. It was a little bigger than a baseball with no bubbles on the inside or scratches on the surface. I began to meditate on the crystal until I saw the smoke filling it—at least that's what it looked like to me. I began to see the vision I was looking for.

Tara was indeed a strong sorceress. I saw her surrounded by creatures that were her helpers. I guess you'd call them angels, but their bodies made them look more like Greek gods. They were coming and going from her as she said her prayers to her Lord. She was surrounded in an aura of blue to white light. She was genuinely concerned about me, according to what I was seeing, and about half the prayers she was offering up was for my increased power. I saw the coven coming to her and being comforted by her. I saw that while her parents were indeed her subordinates, she really did love them. As I was learning all of these things about her I was feeling disappointed in myself for thinking she was not being totally truthful about things. I had gotten a feeling of uneasiness whenever I was around her. Maybe I was just feeling a little intimidated by her since she was way up the ladder in witchcraft, and I was just a rookie. She was right about my abilities, though; I was making incredible progress learning the Craft.

Before I stopped gazing, I saw a vision from the black side of witchcraft. When I began to concentrate on this aspect of the Craft, there suddenly came a bright glowing, radiant being in light blue flowing robes and a silver chrome breastplate. Her skin was as white as the purest driven snow, and she had golden blond hair and piercing blue eyes. She looked up at me from the glass and said, "I am Göndul, the Valkerie. I am the enchanted one. And you, Drahcir, will be my slave for all of time. You will become the hero of your coven, and you will serve the Lord and the Lady. I have decreed it. So may it be."

Into the glass came another figure. It was a man who was built like Mr. Universe with long blond hair and jet black eyes. There was no white in his eyes at all. On his back were wings like that of an angel. He smiled and his teeth were so white they looked unreal, and the canine teeth were long and pointed. I felt compelled to love him in the same way I loved Tara. I was actually lusting after this creature, and for no other reason than just looking at him, I began to get an erection.

An electrical current shot from the crystal and coursed through my body. It shook the hell out of my bones, knocking me backward across the room. I hit a wall and lay there dazed for a few seconds before I got to my feet and looked around the room. I stood up, and I was dizzy from the shock I took. As I regained my wits, I realized I was no longer in my bedroom. It was changed. I was in a large, dark, bricked hallway. The air was warm, stale, and smelled like rotten eggs and on the walls was what appeared to be a soppy wet fungus. The light was so dim here it was really hard to make out exactly what it was. The floor was slippery, as well, and the humidity was stifling. Further down the corridor from where I was, I could see a glow of light. Since there was nothing else to do except stand there, I began to walk toward it. On the floor I could see things moving around my feet, but I couldn't make out exactly what they were. There were voices around me, too. They were whispering some unintelligible gibberish, but they sounded like they were standing right beside me. And, as they whispered, they were sobbing as if their heart had been broken from the news of the death of a loved one. They could not get over the loss even though they begged for the comfort or for the forgiveness.

After the long walk down the corridor, I found two huge heavy wooden doors in the flickering firelight of the torches at the end of the hallway. The mark of the pentagram was etched into each of the doors. The nails, hinges, door handles, and all the other hardware on the door were all made of heavy black wrought iron. From the cracks around the door were beams of light radiating out in brightness as if the source of the light was as bright as the sun. I opened the door slowly and looked inside. The room was completely white to the point I couldn't distinguish the walls from the ceiling. It was filled with light and fog clung to the ground. There was a giant magnificent creature at the center of the room from whom the light was emanating. I looked intently at the face of this creature until my eyes adjusted to the brightness of the light, and I realized it was the woman from the crystal. This was the Valkerie, Göndul, who I had just seen in the glass. The light was coming from a ball that she held in her hand. A feeling of love and hope was flowing from her glowing blue eyes. Her blond hair was shining and blowing in an unfelt wind, and in her hands was a goblet and the ball of light. I approached her cautiously. I knew she knew me, but her immense size was very intimidating.

"Drahcir, why have you been looking in the crystal at the Valkerie?" she asked.

"I was looking for answers, my lady," I replied to her. "I was concerned about my place with Tara, whom I love. I thought perhaps she had mistakenly chosen a traveler who cannot become as powerful in the Craft as she is, no matter how hard he tries."

"The Valkerie chooses only the strongest of mind and spirit and would never approach anyone who was not up to the challenge of learning all the mysteries of the Craft. The Valkerie instructed Tara to choose the traveler. The traveler has powers he has not even realized yet. You, the traveler, will become the most powerful of his kind. The Valkerie has brought you here to gain even more wisdom. In the Craft you have been brought into, there are those benevolent souls who truly believe in the dictum of Wicca. Then there are the warriors of the Craft. You, Drahcir, have been chosen to be a warrior, along with and ruled by, Göndul, the Valkerie. Never again doubt the path you are on or the choice Göndul has made concerning your place in the revolution. You must swear your allegiance to the master. You will dedicate the whole of your being to his service from this time forward, just as the lady, Tara, has done. Do you do this of your own free will?"

"Yes, my lady, I do," I replied at which point she bent down to give me the ball of light. I took it from her. It was only a little bigger than a marble.

"Eat this in remembrance of the goodness the master has shown you. For today he will bestow upon you, Drahcir, the wisdom to discern the deep mysteries of the occult and to be a dark warrior."

I ate the ball of light, and it had a sweet taste. It made me feel very good, like I had more energy than I had ever had before. It made me feel powerful and confident.

"Drink this cup," she said, offering me the goblet. "It is the blood of those who have been martyred for serving the master; martyred by ignorant fools who profess that there is only one kingdom and that it doesn't belong to the master. You must now drink of their blood, and share in their death as they shall share in your life."

I drank expecting to find real blood in the goblet, like I had to do earlier, but instead it was also sweet. It was like a wine, a very strong wine. As soon as I drank it I began to feel drunk.

"And now, Drahcir, you will go into the inner chamber, the holy of holies, to be with the master. You will sit at his feet and learn from him as Göndul has done."

She showed me two doors on the other side of the room. They were huge magnificent doors just as the wooden doors were, but these were made of solid gold. They were adorned with angels falling from heaven and the people below were running and covering their heads. At the top of the door above all the ornate artwork was the head of a dragon, which had the pentagram on its forehead. I opened the door and stepped through.

I entered a room that was large and furnished nicely, but it was not as ethereal as the one I just came from. This looked like some rich guy's library. There was a nice fireplace with a fire blazing away in it. There were beautiful paintings on the walls, and the floor was apparently made of marble. There was red velvet draperies hanging from ceiling to floor and flowers, mostly roses, were in the vases. The air smelled like burning cedar, which is what was probably in the fireplace.

A tall man stood up from the chair in front of the fireplace; a man who appeared to be cultured and educated. He wore a nice pair of khaki pants, a polo sports shirt, and expensive looking dress shoes.

"May I help you?" he asked as he lifted his brandy snifter to his lips.

"I was sent in here by Göndul to see the master. She said I was to learn from him."

"Well, that would be me, I suppose," he said. "I don't go overboard like some people," he said indicating the doors from which I had just come.

I dropped to one knee to bow to him.

"Now, now. We don't have to resort to that," he said, lifting me up from the floor. "You are here to learn from me now. You can do all that homage stuff later, whenever you guys get together for your church. But, before we begin to do this teaching/learning thing, do you understand who I am? I mean, you *do know* who I am, right?"

"You are my lord and master. You are the Prince of Darkness, the Lord of the Air. I will do anything and everything to serve you."

"Why do you say that, Drahcir? Why would you say that knowing that I am Lucifer?"

"To be honest, my lord, between you two guys, you're the one who has proven to me that he is real."

73

He dropped his jaw in a huge grin and his eyes bugged out. "Ha-ha! Ha-ha-ha! I like that answer, my boy! Yes, he just sits up there not doing anything, right? He just lets the world go on doing what it's doing, and he expects everyone to live by his rules. And those rules," he said, rolling his eyes, "don't even get me started. Are you kidding me? How about that very last commandment. Thou shalt not covet thy neighbor's ass. Man! How many times do you think that one has been broken? Every guy on earth has coveted his neighbor's ass or at least his neighbor's wife's ass since...well, believe me it was way, way back there. OK, so, are you ready?" he asked, leading me to a big comfortable looking chair. I sat and yes...it was comfortable. "'Cause I'm gonna go over all of this stuff pretty quickly," he continued. "But don't worry you'll be able to remember all of it. Everything I'm gonna say you'll remember because you have done what the Valkerie told you to do before you came in. You ate and you drank. That's pretty much what it takes to get in here once you've gotten that far. She kinda has a dramatic flair, don't you think?"

We began going over all the mysteries and dark secrets he was going to tell me, and there were a lot of them. He talked to me for several hours. He showed me how to work magic quicker with more accuracy, and he showed me how to increase my divination abilities.

Finally, we stopped for a few minutes and talked about what he would be expecting from me in the future. It was stuff that seemed beyond my ability, but he assured me that when I left this room I would be the second most powerful person in Humble. He also said that he would not leave me alone in the world.

"Tyr! Come here," he said as he called one of his angels to his side. "Drahcir, this is Tyr."

The angel was tall, and when I say tall I mean he was at least 6' 10", with bronze skin and in form much like the vision I had seen in the crystal. Although he didn't have the physical effect on me the way the vision did. "From now on when you cast a spell, you will invoke Tyr. Tyr will do your bidding to my greater glory. Your brothers and sisters in the coven will also enjoy his helpfulness through you, while your enemies will be helpless to defend themselves. That's pretty good, huh? You can finally kick some guy's ass with an invisible force," he chuckled. "Oh, by the way, this is the last time you will actually be able to see him." He reached up and put his hand on the angel's shoulder. "O, but he's a beauty isn't he? He's been with me from the beginning. At one time, I had him set up as a god. The folks in Scandinavia worshipped him as one of the lesser bosses up in Asgard. I'm giving him to you, Drahcir, because you and Tara will be my son and daughter on earth. When you are united I will treat you as my own children. Tara has known how well I can treat my pets for a long time. You can enjoy these benefits, too. Don't think of yourself as just a kid from a small town anymore. You are now royalty. This mark will prove your lineage from now on," he said pointing to my left forearm. I looked and there was a small tattoo of a goat's head on my arm. Like the crescent moon, it too was very detailed. It made the sign of the inverted star with the two horns sticking up, the ears pointing downward, and the goat's beard making the bottom point of the star.

"Now, before I send you back there's something I have to tell you. You should never ever under any circumstances be afraid to try…"

Before he had time to finish what he was saying I found myself being pulled upward through the roof of the room and the light flashing around me was like a lightening storm. The last thing I saw of the master was his grinning face as I flew away.

"Hey! Hey! Are you OK, bubba?"

I felt someone gently slapping me on the face.

"Ricky! Are you OK? Do you want me to go get Dad?"

I looked up and Sheryl was cradling my head in her lap.

"What are you doing?" I asked.

As I tried to rise up I felt a sharp pain on the top of my head.

"What happened?"

"You were talking and that book fell off the bookshelf and hit you on the head. It knocked you out for a second. Are you O.K.?"

"Oh yeah. I'm OK I just want to go to sleep. Thanks for helping me." I tried to play it off like no big deal, but I was confused as hell. How could I have been out for only a second? I remembered every word the master said to me.

"You're welcome. Are you positive you'll be alright?"

"Sure, sure. I'm fine. See ya tomorrow."

"G'night, bubba."

Sheryl left the room, and I picked up the book that fell from the bookshelf. It was nothing amazing, a copy of the poem *Paradise Lost* with commentary. I flipped through the pages and found nothing except the pages I had read at least three times. I turned to put the book back on the shelf, and as I did I saw my reflection in the mirror on the dresser. My left forearm was not the same as when I had entered the room.

CHAPTER 8

For the first time in weeks Tara and I went out, but it wasn't much of a date. We went to the local theater, the Jewel. It was run by the Ivey sisters—a couple of old ladies who were very strict in enforcing the rules.

These were the rules in a nut shell:

After you paid for the ticket you were allowed to come in and watch the movie. The purchase of refreshments was optional, but any of the following infractions was punishable by expulsion from the theater. If you were found guilty after the second warning you were banned from the theater for two weeks. The eight inexcusable offences, according to the Ivey sisters, were:

Running in the theater

Talking during the movie

Throwing the previously mentioned refreshments at other moviegoers

Clapping for the bad guy

Clapping too enthusiastically for the good guy

Holding hands

Putting an arm around someone (boyfriend/girlfriend)

Kissing (strictly forbidden)

And if a young lady was found allowing a curious young man to cop a feel, it was punishable by expulsion for an indefinite period of time for both individuals involved. And the young lady was branded forever after as one of the town tramps.

Tara and I got to the second warning on item numbers two, six, seven, and eight. We thought about going for the big enchilada, but this was like *it* as far as nightlife in Humble. We might want to come back again sometime.

The movie was only so-so. It was *Rasputin: The Mad Monk,*

which some of the people in the theater actually thought was going to be a movie about an ape that goes crazy and hopefully John Wayne would come in to save the day.

Humble was pretty big on John Wayne. He shot parts of the movie *The Hell Fighters* at Moonshine Hill. Almost all of the parts that were shot in Humble were edited out of the movie except for the part where they're supposed to be flying over Canada. All the trees you see in that shot is Humble. We're all pretty proud of those five seconds of film. All the little shops all over town had a picture of John Wayne hanging on the wall. For a while it was like, "We don't have Astrodomes and fancy hotels and restaurants in Humble, but we had John Wayne, by God!"

After the movie, we went down to the park and sat in the swings for a while. It was only four or five blocks and if you have ever seen a small town park, you've seen the one in Humble. At that time it had no fence around it. I think that was because they wanted anyone who wanted to swing or slide to just be able to come in and do what they wanted. Of course, now they realize if people were still allowed to come in anytime of the day or night to swing and/or slide these pieces of equipment would wear out in no time flat—say fifteen or twenty years. That's an expense, and what about the manpower it takes to patrol a half acre piece of open landscape? We have to think about these things, people.

Sorry. I got off on a tangent, there.

Anyway, Tara and I were at the park sitting on the swings in the cold evening air. It was now mid-February and leaves were still falling off the trees. The leaves that had already fallen off were blowing across the park resembling some sort of chaotic race as they went tumbling over the grass. People were getting in the spirit of Valentine's Day with hearts and little cupids taped up in their windows and hanging from their trees.

The perfume of the night filled me with an incredible sense of euphoria. I was beginning to feel quite giddy, and I guess it was due to the trees releasing oxygen into the air that I was not really concentrating on what Tara was talking about. All I could think about was how I was absolutely head over heels in love with her. I looked at her that night, her body swinging slowly back and forth with a background of silhouetted trees and a clear, starry, moonlit night, thinking that this was the picture I would always have of her in my mind's eye. Her brown hair shining in the moonlight—her blue eyes sparkling as she spoke—the way she not only pronounced words, but the way she shaped her mouth when she said them—the wrinkle of her nose right around the nostrils as she laughed. I wanted to remember all of these little things about her. I knew if I surprised her and she laughed a little when she heard my voice, then she was glad to see me and that she wanted to talk. I knew what her favorite drink was. I knew what music she liked. I knew what kind of dog, car, house, sport, perfume, and shoes she liked. I knew when we were sitting on the couch or in the car if she rested her head back on my arm she wanted to be kissed. I wanted to know her better than I had known anyone else ever before. When I did, I never knew anyone else as well again. There were a thousand and one things that endeared her to me, and it all boiled down to this: I knew that I loved her and I knew that she loved me.

The entire time I had been etching this vision of her in my mind, she had been talking about the pathetic arrangement of the music we were practicing for the spring concert. She was a bit of a purist when it came to symphonic music. Our school band wasn't bad at all; in fact, I thought it was very good. The talent to play what she wanted, I believe, was there. However, the proper instrumentation was lacking. We had no string section at all, only brass, woodwinds, and percussion. Ah, but we had heart. And we had an excellent director, Mr. Robert Wylie, who invariably insisted on calling me Richard, even though he knew I didn't like that. OK, actually, he would call me that whenever I would act like an ass. There were some things Bob and I didn't see eye to eye on, but I still thought he was a jam-up director.

She was going on about how we needed violins playing in the main piece we were practicing. It was Wagner's *Elsa's Procession*, one of her personal favorites. I have to admit, we played it far above average. When we played it at the UIL concert contest we not only aced it, the judges were actually moved to having tears in their eyes.

In mid sentence, I grabbed her off of her swing and kissed her such a deep, passionate kiss I prayed she could feel how much I loved her.

When at last we came up for air, I said to her, "Tara, I love you far beyond the ability to express in mere words. You are my first thought in the morning when I get up and my last thought at night when I lie down. In between that time, I think about you only whenever my heart beats. You have brightened my life by just being in it. I love you in three ways, and I want you to always remember this…I love you in three ways: deeply, passionately, and eternally. And if, for whatever reason, I would be forced to mask the truth, it is you I will love, still, forevermore. I'm just a poor boy from a small town, but you would make me the richest man in this whole world if you would marry me. Will you, Tara? Will you marry me?"

She looked at me with eyes that spoke volumes before she said a word. The bluest, sweetest eyes I had ever seen displayed confidence in this answer. "This is something I have thought about for quite some time, Drahcir. When I give you this answer I want you to understand it has been given serious thought, and that I am not saying this flippantly. You're a great guy, and I believe the master has wonderful plans for you in the future. I, too, care for you far beyond the ability for mortals to convey. I would rather die than to live without you. You stole my heart the first day I saw you, and you have been in my every thought since. I would be very happy to be united with you. We will have a Wiccan handfasting ceremony, and I would be honored to be your wife."

I couldn't believe the words I was hearing. It was the first time I had heard her speak so sincerely. This was the most wonderful thing I could have ever imagined.

"When should we tell your parents?" I asked.

"We will tell them at the same time we tell all of our brothers and sisters. We'll tell them at the next meeting. And then, at the celebration of Ostara on March 21st we will be handfasted."

"You know, most guys have to ask the father for the hand of their daughter. Don't you think I should ask him?"

"You want to ask for my hand from my father?"

"Yes. Don't you think that would be the courteous thing to do?"

"You don't remember what the Father said to you when he was putting Tyr as your special angel? He said, *'I'm giving him to you, Drahcir, because you and Tara will be my son and daughter on earth. When you are united I will treat you as my own children.'* He has already given you permission to become united with me."

"Baby," I chuckled and rolled my eyes, "I'm not at all surprised you know about that, but *how* do you know? If it wasn't for this tattoo I wouldn't even believe it really happened," I said, pulling up my shirt sleeve to show her the mark.

"You saw the Lady, darlin', don't you remember? She is Göndul, and my Lady never keeps any secrets from me," she said as she pulled her pants down exposing her behind. On her left cheek was a mark like the one I had on my arm. "I asked him to put it there so it wouldn't show too much."

An intense bright light shown around us, and we were blinded as we looked into it. We couldn't see who was holding the light, but we could hear the voices of several guys. We felt strongly that they were not here to exchange pleasantries. I assumed they were drunken rednecks.

Most of the teenagers in Humble during the '70s were divided into two major groups. Notice that I'm not saying gangs because back then there were no gangs in the sense of gangs today. Most guys had the guts to fight their own battles. They didn't need to hide behind a façade of being tough because their homies would help them kick some ass. Anyway, the two groups were the surfers (yes, there are surfers in Texas) and the kickers (a word that is short and considerably more polite than using the complete shit kickers in reference to cowboys.)

It was a foregone conclusion that on the weekends the surfers were going to jump into their wet suits and head for either Galveston or Freeport, and the kickers would stick around town, get drunk, and fight. If they couldn't find someone to fight they would just fight each other. Every once in awhile they would get bold (which involved getting drunk) and go into Houston to either Mom's Café or the Crystal Pistol diner and look for some queers to roll. That activity slowed down considerably after a few of them picked up a federal officer and rolled him by mistake. There was some time paid in Huntsville for that one. I always wished the kickers would all just gravitate over to Gilley's in Pasadena and annoy each other over there instead of the nighttime people of Humble.

But, no, here they were trying to do whatever they thought they were going to do with Tara and me. Their voices were not unknown to me. It was Jerry, Bobby, and David. All were the stereotypical good 'ol boys, big in FFA and football. The only difference was they didn't go by some moniker like Bubba, Booger, or Moose. Well, there was a guy who went by Moose, but it wasn't any of these guys.

They walked up to us within about twenty feet or so, and unfortunately for us, we were down wind. Don't get me wrong, I like beer and an occasional taste of bourbon or wine, but these guys must have been drinking sheep dip or something. They reeked is what I'm talking about.

"Well, well, well. What do we have here?" Jerry said with the light still glaring in our eyes. "Why, it's Mr. Music Man, Ricky Stevens. You sure can toot good, Rick. Every time I run the ball in for a touchdown and you guys start playing the fight song, I know you're up there tootin' with all your fart."

It was Jerry holding the flashlight because Bobby and David circled around to flank us. These two were decked out in all of their finery. One had on a button down cowboy shirt that had the sleeves torn off and wearing a straw cowboy hat that looked like he may have used it for a pillow a time or two because it was a beat up mess. The other one had on a wife beater T-shirt—you know, the kind of undershirt that has a couple of straps across the shoulders for sleeves—some people call it a muscle shirt. He was sporting a red baseball type hat with big white polka dots on it. The balance of their ensemble was made up the standard blue jeans and cowboy boots that were so pointed you could squash a roach hiding in a corner. I damn near laughed thinking about how they thought they were scaring us. They looked like such big, bad hombres.

"And who is this with you, Mr. Music Man? Who is this little heifer? Why, she's a cute little ol' gal. Yeah, she's cuter than a bug's belly button. You want some of this here, sweet thang?" he asked holding up a jelly jar half full of what appeared to be White Lightening. At the same time he finally pointed the flashlight away from our eyes. His ensemble was worse than the other two. He was bare headed and had on a pair of overalls, which were gapped open on each side to the waist, and what if anything, he had on under those was anyone's guess. He was also wearing cowboy boots, but the tops of these had been split down the middle, front and rear, so that he could stuff the pants leg into the inside half of the boot top and let the other side dangle out of the outside half of the boot top. I assume this had some sort of practical application in the world of redneckdom. Possibly it kept one from getting cow shit on ones pant's cuff while strolling through the pasture. He continued to address Tara saying, "This is some of the smoothest 'shine you'll ever come across, ain't that right, boys?"

"Oh yeah, it sure is, sweetie. See it makes my dick real hard," Bobby said, trying to unzip his pants. The only thing that kept us from seeing his chubby little fella right then was that he was too drunk to find the zipper key.

"Look, Jerry, y'all need to just turn right on around and go back to where ever it was y'all came from. We didn't come out here looking for any trouble."

"Oh, is that right, Mr. Band Geek? Well, how about if you just shut the hell up, 'cause we didn't come out here to talk to your sorry ass." He turned and smiled at Tara. "We came out here to see her. Yeah, that's right. We came out here to see her...titties. Come on, honey, show us them titties and...well, we'll just have to see what happens from there."

"I think you boys should do what Rick said and leave before something bad happens. Don't you think that would be a good idea?" Tara asked.

David pulled a revolver from his blue jeans belt line and said, "I think a good idea would be for you to just jump nekked, right now," he said, cocking the hammer back. "And throw me them panties when you get 'em off."

"David, you stupid little twerp," I said confidently. "Point your little gun over there and shoot between Jerry's feet."

Without hesitation he pointed and shot hitting squarely between Jerry's feet, who simultaneously pissed in his pants. Bobby lunged at Tara who held up one of her hands knocking ol' Bob several feet backward from the point he started. David came at me with the revolver still in his hand. I willed him to stop dead in his tracks, which he did just as Jerry was about to put me in a headlock. I hoisted him into the air and threw him back to the point he was before he got the idea to rush me.

When Bobby and Jerry stood up I said, "Gentlemen, all of you need to fall in line and strip naked right here, right now." Which they did. Now we saw Bobby's little fella, and it was exactly that, just a wee little fella.

They were standing there at attention with a look on their faces like, *What the hell is going on here.* It was pretty obvious their buzz was long gone, and they were fully aware of what was happening.

"Now, guys," I said, trying to keep a straight face, "do you see what a mess you've gotten into by not listening to Sylvia and me? So now, when I tell you to, you're going to walk the length of Main Street, starting right here, and walk to the railroad tracks about a mile and a half away."

"I want you to walk right down the middle of the street," Tara continued. "You will not get out of the way of cars. You will be marching like cute little band geeks and discussing, loudly enough for everyone to hear, how ignorant you are."

"Every ten seconds I want both Jerry and Bobby to slap David's ass real hard three times." I further instructed them.

Tara walked over behind David and said softly in his ear, "By the way, I don't *ever* wear panties."

She walked around them like she was inspecting her troops. Well, she *was* inspecting her troops, and all they could do was to just stand there.

"My goodness, boy," she said to Bobby, "I've seen more meat than that in a flower shop. And what is that, scabs or something? Lemme give you a hint, sonny boy, hand lotion. Use some hand lotion when you jack off."

Next she went over to David. "Is that all there is? Is it drawn up or something, or is it always like that? It looks like a little egg sitting in a bird nest."

"There is *no* mistake," she said to Jerry, "your parents are definitely *not* Jewish. Look at that pathetic thing. It looks like a wrinkly old carrot."

I wouldn't swear to it, but I thought I saw Jerry's chin quiver just a little when she made the observation of his John Thomas.

"OK, guys," she continued, "now when I snap my fingers I want all three of you to march in place starting with your left foot. Every time I snap my fingers, your left foot will come down. OK? March!" she said as she started to snap her fingers. "Click, step, click, step, click, step! OK, good, now walk!"

Away they went down Main Street yelling as loud as they could, "We is ignorant, ain't we Bobby!?"

"We shore is David! Who you think is the most ignorant, Jerry!?"

Pow! Pow! Pow! David's cheeks wiggled like Jell-O when they administered his three swats.

"Y'all both is purty ignorant, but I'm more ignorant than either one of y'all!"

"Naw, you ain't neither!"

"Oh, yeah I am!"

Pow! Pow! Pow!

And so it went until they were out of sight. They got almost to the end of Main Street when the law finally picked them up. I bet that was one crazy interrogation.

Tara and I began walking again down Old River Road toward the San Jacinto River. It was a long way from the park to the river, and we talked and made plans on when the hand-fasting ceremony would be and when we would tell everyone. We walked all the way down Old River Road until we ran out of hardtop and we found ourselves on the dirt road in the woods just before the river.

The moonlight was sifting down through the trees with a backdrop of a navy blue sky. There were only a few silvery clouds— nothing that was going to obscure the stars. The ground fog roamed in and out through the trees like lost ghosts looking for their haunt. It was a very eerie sight.

As we stood there looking through the fog-laden woods I thought I saw someone dart from one tree to another as if trying to hide from us. We walked along for a little while longer, and I saw the person again, much clearer this time. It was a girl in a white flowing dress, which gave her a ghostly appearance amid the fog floating around her.

"Did you see that?" I asked.

Tara sighed and looked disappointed that our alone time was over. "I've seen her often. Is this the first time you've seen her?"

"Well yeah, it's the first time I've seen her. What do you mean you've seen her often? Do you have someone trailing you all the time? Is she stalking you or what?"

"She is Cassandra, and she is my rival from a coven in Massachusetts. She watches me all the time, just as I also watch her."

"Why is she watching you?"

"She's watching me because she is jealous of you. She is also mentoring a young man, but he just isn't as adept as you."

"OK, so why doesn't she just come over here and introduce herself?"

"Well, that's probably because she doesn't feel up to getting her ass kicked tonight. For another thing, that is not really her you are seeing over there. Cassandra is actually in Salem. She's doing a little astral projecting. It's a way we mess with each other's head."

"Is she a part of the old witch heritage of Salem?"

"I hear her family goes way back in the history of the area. Those poor old bible thumpers way back there didn't really have a clue though, you know? They were burning up a bunch of sweet little old ladies and killing off a bunch of old men because if the neighbor's cow died it must have been because old Josh Shoebuckle next door put a hex on it. Or if someone caught one of the town's girls naked in the daylight, she must be a witch. All of the real witches didn't let themselves get caught, and there were a lot of them."

"So why does Cassandra watch us all the time?"

"She wants my position, and she wants you," Tara said, looking at me in a way I suppose was to see if I would have a reaction. I had none.

"She wants you because you are the gifted one between the two travelers," she continued. "If she could get you to support her, she would try to take my position away from me as the next High Priestess of North America."

"I thought you were a shoe in. You mean it isn't guaranteed that you will be the next High Priestess?"

"It will come down to a battle for control of the position. Cassandra is very strong, but I know I can beat her. I need you beside me to win and I know I will win. When I do, you and I will be the power in North America."

I saw Cassandra watching us from a distance. Her ghostly form darted in and out of the shadows and between trees. She watched us all the way down to the bank of the river.

From the bank where we stood, we could see the other shore. It was as black as the one we were standing on. All we could really see were the treetops as they swayed in the gentle night breeze and the moonlight as it was broken up on the river waters. The water was gently lapping up to the bank where we were and a few Sandpipers ran along the beach pecking at the sand, gobbling up some little delicious tidbit, and scurrying away down the bank. The only sound they made was an occasional squeal. Other than that, it was a quiet night along the San Jacinto.

When we turned we found Cassandra was standing not two feet from us. She was a devastating beauty with long jet-black hair, pale white skin, red pouting lips, and piercing green eyes. Her eyes glowed in the darkness softly, and they were trained on me the entire time. The white flowing robe she wore was clinging to a well-proportioned body that moved absolutely unrestrained under the sheer material.

"Hello, Tara. Who is this with you tonight?" she asked, her eyes still going over my body as if she were seeing right through my clothes.

"You know who this is, Cassandra."

"Yes, I know Drahcir. I was hoping you would display an unusual side of yourself and have the courtesy to introduce us in the proper Southern hospitable way," she said to Tara.

Turning to me she introduced herself, "Drahcir, I am very happy to meet you. As I am sure she has mentioned to you, I am Cassandra of Salem."

She held out her hand for me to kiss and I was about to favor her. However, a highly agitated witch pulled her hand away from my lips.

"You filthy bitch! How dare you come here and try to charm my fiancée right out from under my nose. You leave this place or I'll…"

"You'll what, Tara?" Cassandra giggled. "What are you going to do to me since I am not even really here?"

"I'll come to you on your own turf in the flesh, and we'll see once and for all who the strongest witch is."

Tara's eyes were glowing, too. They were glowing like a raging fire.

"You won't do any such thing, baby girl." Cassandra giggled. "You don't quite have all the strength you need, but soon, sweetie, soon I'll be strong enough to deliver the message that will rock the heavens, and your church will come tumbling down," she said as she reached over and gave me a gentle squeeze in the crotch.

The anger spewed forth from Tara and she pointed a finger shaking with hate at her enemy. At once a bolt of lightening hit the spot where she stood followed by an ear splitting roar of thunder. Cassandra laughed at the agitation she had caused. That was what she had come to do in the first place and having accomplished that she vanished from sight leaving only the echo of laughter.

I was, of course, the innocent bystander in this whole encounter. This fracas had nothing to do with me. At least that is what I thought. As it turned out, I was the central figure in the squabble that occurred just then. As a matter of fact, I was the rouge of the evening, it seemed.

"You just stood there and let her pinch you on the dick! You want her, don't you? You thought she had a cute ass, and you want to jump in the sack with her as soon as I'm not around, is that it? Well, let me tell you something, *Mr. Drahcir,* I picked you out of about one hundred other people I thought would be a good witch. I made you what you are today. And you're just that. A good witch. Is this the way you thank me?"

"Tara."

"You shut up, you son of a bitch. I'm not through with you yet," she screamed through tears. "I thought you loved me. I thought we were going to be hand-fasted. You're just a…a…a whore. You don't care about me. You don't care about the Craft or anything."

"Tara, I didn't do anything, honey," I said as I took her by her arms to try to settle her down. "She reached over here so quickly I didn't have time to respond. And why would I want that old shriveled up hag, anyway? I have the best looking witch in the whole world."

She smiled and was beginning to settle down now. I held her close to my chest. "Really?" she smiled through tears.

"Really. You're so pretty. You know who you look like? Ali McGraw. You look a whole lot like Ali McGraw. You could be twin sisters, you look so much alike."

"I do?" she sniffed, wiping tears from her eyes and trying to muster a faint smile.

"Oh, yeah. You two could be sisters, I'm telling you."

"Really? Who's Ali McGraw?"

"Baby doll, you really, really need to see some movies sometime."

We sat on the shore there on the San Jacinto and listened to the lapping of the waves and the sound of the birds squealing and flying overhead. We sat on the sandy shore of the river discussing our life plans and fantasies, fantasies of living in a Swiss villa on an Alpine mountainside, driving an exotic car like an MGB/GT, and having a St. Bernard dog. We sat in the moonlight as the stars in icy silence kept watch over us. We discussed the distant future on the banks of the river that night until the eastern sky began to get rosy with the approaching dawn. Then we made our way back to our individual homes and to our individual beds.

CHAPTER 9

I n the weeks that followed we sharpened our skills in practicing on the local towns people. We found the track team to be an amusing bunch of fellows who were at our disposal, more or less. All of us who were members of the church and were in band, would sit together.

I sort of enjoyed going to the track meets because the band didn't have to participate on a mandatory basis there. We did have a few instruments there as a pep band, but we didn't have to march or anything retarded like that. Halftime at football games was the only part of band I didn't like. I still can't see how anyone can be expected to play truly good music while walking around in a predetermined pattern. Not only is the victim, I mean student, expected to play the music as well as can be performed, while making a vain attempt to hold the instrument steady, but they were expected to remember to ensure that the arch of the right foot always lay across each five-yard line when those points were reached, maintain a straight line across the field, make each turn in the correct place on the field and to do so with snap. That always made it look so sharp. I thought marching band was the most absolute waste of time, musically, that I ever had to go through.

After we had played a few of our little novelty tunes at the track meet for the entire crowd to o-o-o and a-a-h at, we were given a little free time to do whatever. We usually "whatevered" all over the track guys. It was great. Tara made one guy fall over every hurdle he came to. Bres had our long jumper trip and fall right at the point of taking that big leap into space. Owlen blinded our shot put guys so they couldn't see where they were supposed to let the thing go, which sent all the judges scrambling for cover. They didn't know where it was going to land. They just knew if they stayed in the same spot it would more than likely land on their head. Luna had a good one. There was one guy that would run anchor in the mile relay, and when he would win he would drop the baton on the ground and strut around with his closed fists in the air like "Hey! Am I bad or what?" He was just a little big headed on the track and off. Luna fixed it so when he raised his hands after a win these huge crows would come swooping in and dive bomb him until he would be running around to get away from them. Everybody in the bleachers thought that it was hilarious.

We picked on the jocks off of the field, too. Remember Astra's fascination with Mr. Queer Football Star? His desire for those with outdoor plumbing was stronger than the love spell she cast on him, so she put a whammy on him one day. All day while walking between classes all he could do was walk up and down the hall telling everyone around, "I'm hell. I'm hell." Over and over he said it and couldn't stop even when Mr. Barr (who was another story altogether—does the word rhinovore conjure up any kind of disgusting habit he might have had?) stopped him and asked why he was saying that. All he could answer was, "I'm hell." At which point Mr. Barr escorted him to Stick's (a.k.a. Principal Smith) office and pressed his hams a few times with an ass-paddle. That was the sort of thing that was common in those times—corporal punishment. He told him to grab his ankles making the muscles of the glutamous maximus (his ass) real tight so when the paddle came in contact with it forcefully and repeatedly it hurt very badly. This is again the voice of experience talking here. Astra finally did get her jollies from the gay football guy. Just not the way she originally wanted to.

The other group of people that were great to jack with was the teachers. There was this one jerk wad history teacher, Mr. Davis, who loved to exert his authority over the students. One day one of the girls in the class needed to go to the restroom. He refused to let her go. A few minutes later she approached him again and again he said no. Once more she came to his desk and asked to go to the restroom, and he told her to go sit down and not to ask again. He informed her that she could hold it until the end of the class. Instead of returning to her desk she burst into tears, lost control, and embarrassed herself in front of the entire classroom, as well as the school, after word got around. I hated that teacher for that. He had absolutely no right in trying to control the function of her bladder. So, one day I decided that he needed to know just how that felt.

We were standing near the restrooms one day when I noticed him coming down the hall in a rather hasty manner. Telepathically I began to put people and things in his way. He had to duck this and dodge that while keeping his eyes fixed on the restroom door. I knew he really needed to go. When he got to me I stood in his way and asked him, "Mr. Davis, I was wondering. Do you tape record your lecture every night before you come to work, or do you tape the lecture given to the first class of the day, and then just play it back for the remaining classes while you sit with your feet propped up eating an apple and checking out the pussies of the girls on the front row? I've seen you looking up their skirts, you sly old dog, you."

"How dare you insinuate such a thing. I don't have time for this right now. Get to your class and leave me alone," he ordered me as he tried to push me aside.

"Oh no, sir. I don't think so. I want you to stand right there until I say you can go."

His shoes became fastened to the ground and his feet fastened to his shoes. You can imagine the look of shock that swept over his face. It was glorious.

I bent close to his left ear and said in a half whisper, "No, sir, I think you should stand there and piss in your pants until your drawers are soppy wet and your slacks are darkly stained. You stand there and piss and stink and be a laughing stock to your peers until your damn shoes fill up. I want you to piss so long and hard that people will not be able to believe that all that piss came out of one man, you fucking son of a bitch."

Much to his chagrin the other teachers, as well as the students, found many moments of mirth and merriment watching him stand stark still in the hallway and piss down both legs. The puddle surrounded him and a stream ran down the hallway. The janitor, curious, was not at all amused.

CHAPTER 1Ø

With all the time I had been spending with my new brothers and sisters, I hadn't spent time with hardly anyone else. Bear, Go, Woody, Bar-B-Q…they were all avoiding me because they thought I was being too good for them. It wasn't that I felt that way at all. It's just that all the studying and the time I was spending with Sylvia left me practically no time left. What time I did have apart from them I needed to spend with my blood relatives, my sister and brother—Sheryl and John. Dad was really his normal self only to a little greater degree. He never got out of the kickback chair except to eat lunch or dinner. Mom…it was like Mom had gotten a lobotomy. She was always sunshiny, smiles…the world was just a big bowl of bubbles to her. She never questioned anything any of us did. It scared the hell out of Sheryl.

But, Don was still around, and he and I would hang out a little every now and then. He enjoyed the little parlor tricks I would do for him, like light his smoke with the tip of my finger or magically pull a joint from behind his ear. He liked that one most of all. He didn't know what was going on with my life, but he was a little upset that I hadn't been around.

One day we were at the marina debating on whether or not we should borrow someone's johnboat for a little cruise on the river.

"So I guess you and Sylvia are getting sort of serious, huh? Did she ever teach you how to meditate?" he said, looking down at the helpless and unoccupied johnboat.

"Oh, yeah, she taught me, all right. She's taught me more than that, though."

"Like what?" I think he was expecting some sexy details.

"Life," I said as we untied it from the wet dock.

He screwed up his face, sneered his dissatisfaction, and said, "Oh,

94

man. Are you gonna get all crazy with it, now?"

"Don, there is more to life than just the physical aspect."

"Oh, yeah, there you go with it."

We stepped into the boat, Don grabbing one paddle and I had the other.

"Listen. You can't look at things in only the here and now. Everything that is true is not necessarily tangible. There is the spiritual aspect and the metaphysical."

"Ah, Jeez, man. You're really eaten up with all that stuff, aren't you? Look, I know you were like that before, all artsie-fartsie, but now…I'm gonna tell you, Rick. You're getting to be a real pain in the ass. You used to be pretty cool, for a band geek. Can't you just hang out and admire my ability to attract females with my boyish good looks and god-like physique?"

He stood there looking at me striking a Mr. Universe pose with one eyebrow cocked and sweeping his invisible moustache with his finger.

"Look if you're gonna wipe your nose, at least do it the proper way like your momma taught you. Use your sleeve."

"Don't be talking 'bout my momma," he joked as he splashed water on me with his paddle.

Splashing water back on him I replied, "And I might be artsie but I am *not* fartsie."

"Oh, yes you are, sometimes. You do get kinda fartsie."

"Well, maybe sometimes," I confessed.

We were getting out of the cove and into the river.

"That's usually on pinto bean day at school," Don said.

"Pinto bean day isn't as bad as lima bean and boiled egg day, though," I countered.

"True. True." He paused, taking a hit off a joint. "Remember when I made that kid throw up on the bus that day? All the windows were up because it was so cold and I cut a *BAD* one." He laughed as he passed me the doob. "He threw his cookies right down there on the bus floor."

I couldn't help but laugh. That was about the best true fart story around. I witnessed it. It was true. It was a legend around the school for a time. Don Cox, be careful or he'll gas ya.

We spent the rest of the day reminiscing about the days when we were in junior high and all the trouble we would get into and the things we did and never got caught at. The best thing we ever did AND got caught at was peeking in the girls' locker room in the gym. We got a full minute or minute and a half look before the coach caught us. He popped our asses good for that one. Oh, but what price is too dear for glory? We had dared to live the reality of every other schoolboy's dream.

We ended the day by returning the johnboat to where we had found it, and when we had gotten back to the neighborhood, Don went his way and I went mine.

CHAPTER 11

I was no longer living at home. I told Tara I wanted to move out of my parents' home, and she saw to it that I was supplied with a furnished trailer on the property. When Tara came over we would meditate for hours. It wasn't the calm quiet mediation we practiced one day on the beach at Galveston. It was a cosmic, psychedelic experience. When we joined hands to begin there was a bright blue light that would illuminate the room, and it would pulsate throughout the experience. We left our bodies and traveled to many different places. Some of the places were just places she wanted to show me, but the majority of the time we went to see what Cassandra was doing. I never liked to go there. I felt like something terrible would happen to us. We never let her know of our presence, but she knew.

She had her lackey with her most of the time. He seemed to me to be a slow-witted buffoon. Why she would pick someone like him to mentor was beyond my understanding. Perhaps it was because he was well built. He certainly didn't have the mental capacity to retain the complicated spells that Tara and I had mastered. I asked Tara several times why she didn't simply go ahead and squash her like the bug she was. She would never give me a straight answer. The only thing she said about it was that the time and the stars would have to be right.

As the remaining weeks went on we continued with the spells for strength. The dogs and cats that were sacrificed were no longer bothering me. I was getting stronger with every dead animal. It was true that the slower they died, the more of their life force we were gaining. The more pain they experienced while in the throes of death, the more exhilarating the life force felt entering our bodies. It was an electrifying feeling, and the thought crossed my mind that this was only the blood of *animals*.

We were developing more and more as an organized coven. There were several members of the church that didn't belong to our elite group, such as Tara's mom and dad and a few others that were only interested in communing with nature, being with a lot of other people, and dancing around naked and junk like that. They were not even close to us as far as performing black magic. We, the thirteen, were all into the master level of casting spells. It was really fun to use the magic to our advantage. It seemed like for so long the people around town had looked down on my family and me, and now I could have some revenge. The rest of the guys had their own form of entertainment.

One of their favorite forms of entertainment was to morph into one another's appearance and confuse people by walking away in one direction and the visage of the same person walk up from another direction. On one special occasion all of the girls except Tara, which included Chakkra, Astra, Luna, Owlen, and Aura, took turns morphing into Luna and sharing her boyfriend. They said it's as close to swinging as they were going to be able to get to until they were married. The old boy they were sharing probably wouldn't even have cared if they did all bang him as who they really were. They thought it was just more fun to deceive him like this. It would have gone a lot farther, probably, except for one afternoon when Chakkra, as Luna, went over to get crazy with him and wound up getting *really* crazy. She related the event in this way:

It started as a normal afternoon delight. After some small talk and a little iced tea he led her into the bedroom where they began to get ferociously passionate by kissing, groping, feeling, and sucking. Their hands were frantically running over each other's body feeling every protrusion and crevice. Chakkra playfully squeezed his bulging erection as he fondled her soft supple breasts for a few seconds and then reached under her skirt and between her legs to run his hands over her panties. Underneath them he felt the downy silk of pubic hair and the moistness of her vagina. Finally they stripped each other while continuing with all of the above activity and continued in the bed with the furious foreplay. He was going down on Chakkra,

burying his nose in the softness of her womanhood, and she was
going down on him like it was her own until he was at the brink of
explosion. She got on top of him and as he entered her she began to
come in a flurry of spasmodic waves. As he began to come he looked
up at the body that was on top of him who was morphing from Luna
to Astra to Owlen to Aura to herself and back to Luna in rapid
succession. Darkness filled the room. She said she thought the look
of terror in his eyes was the best part. It was such a rush to see the look
of perfect terror in his face, and she had never felt a climax that was
so intense. She continued to morph throughout the climax ending in
a face of a decaying corpse. The boy she was screwing screamed in
horror as he saw the vision of rotting flesh falling from her face onto
his. Finally, Chakkra disappeared as if she had never even been in the
room. In disbelief he got out of the bed on weak, wobbly knees. He
walked over to the bedroom mirror and saw between his own legs
where there had been a rather respectful penis there was now a black
shriveled mess that resembled a way over ripened banana. As it fell
to the floor he again screamed and looked down at his maligned boy
toy—to find it in tact. He thought he heard a giggle and the bedroom
door opened and closed by itself.

Astra, Owlen, Aura, and especially Luna were not at all happy
with the report. Their play time with the "stove pipe," as they
affectionately referred to him, had also come to an end. They didn't
worry about him telling anyone, though. Who the hell would believe
him? There were plenty of other puppets they could play with. It was
just that Luna really sort of liked this guy. At school he began to
avoid her. Go figure.

The men in the group were of a more serious nature, including
me. We were a powerful bunch in Humble in '73. We were not to be
taken lightly, and yet, there came a direct threat upon our church one
day.

The Evangelistic Church of Humble had brazenly declared that if
a coven of witches were ever discovered in Humble, the members of
their church would declare a spiritual war against it and drive it out
of town. That didn't set too well with us. For one thing, they didn't

know that we were already here, and for another thing, they were already making threats against us.

Beginning that week we started attending that church on a regular basis. We sat in the middle section of the church praying the entire time to our Lord to send his angels to disrupt the meeting. It was a magnificent success. In the succeeding weeks the atmosphere became dense in the church building, a feeling of depression and futility was prevalent throughout each service, attendance fell off more and more each week. The young junior high and high school girls of the church were becoming pregnant, and the church members fought against each other, falsely accusing each other's children of wrong doing. They really did go on witch-hunts, so to speak. But, they were ignorant of the fact that witch-hunts don't matter in Christianity. They were on missions to battle the enemy and doing things Jesus Christ would not have even thought of doing, such as lambasting the music that was labeled Christian rock and roll, and saying they could hear the demons screeching away in it—trying to fight for rights as Christians—down right raising hell when John Lennon made that silly little comment that everyone took too literally. Did Christ indicate that his followers should be militant instead of pacifistic? Did Paul write something about the right of every Christian to go blow up abortion clinics and to be judgmental about anything that didn't set well with some money-hungry TV evangelists? Did I miss that one or what? And then, (and this was the best of them all) the members of the Evangelistic Church were instructed to visualize their financial success—to name it and claim it—that in itself bordered right on the brink of witchcraft.

After a few weeks of our attendance, the time came when they realized that the enemy had infiltrated them when we got one of the little old church ladies to ask for permission to speak in front of the congregation. She was a dear little thing, but hardly frail. She was rather stocky to be in her late 70s. On several occasions she asked to testify, and she would talk and talk and talk. During Humble's oil boom days she said her little brother and she would go around to the oilmen's bunkhouses and collect their wash and do it for a nickel a load. When she spoke she sounded like she was on her last breath, yet she reportedly ate a pound of bacon everyday for breakfast.

On this occasion she was allowed to speak, as usual, and she went up before the crowd. As she turned to speak, her face contorted into an unrecognizable mask and the obscenities that spewed forth were enough to make a sailor blush. The congregation was shocked into a paralysis. The stink of rotting eggs pervaded the room and the temperature dropped about twenty degrees. She was screaming their shortcoming to them, calling them everything from assholes to whores. At the end of her tirade she threw her head and arms back as if nailed to a cross and began to float up off of the floor and to hover over the awe stricken assembly. They could now easily see that at some point before her speech she had discarded her underwear and was now sporadically defecating on a few of the more unfortunate folks in the crowd.

Judex, Bragi, Bres, Sigurd, Styx, Raven, and I were laughing our asses off when the preacher finally snapped as to where all the shenanigans, monkeyshines, and tom-fooleries were coming from. He expeditiously expelled us from the church in the name of Jesus. (Is that something Jesus would have done, I wonder?)

"You have each sold your souls to Satan, and for what? A season of pleasure on earth? Young men, after this life will come your final judgment: everlasting damnation into the pit created for Satan and his angels. There you will be tormented by fire, excluded from fellowship with any other soul, and most sorrowfully—beyond the reach of the love of God. I beg you to keep in mind that as long as you have air left in your lungs and a life on this earth, you can turn to Christ for the forgiveness of your sins. I urge you to do so, most emphatically."

When we found our way outside we lit up a smoke and discussed the course of action we should take. We talked about what he had said. We agreed that it was from the conviction of his heart that he spoke these words to us, and those words spoken were meant to be for our own good. We decided to show our appreciation. We thanked him for his kind words by casting a spell calling for his wooden frame church building to burn to the ground. All of the holy (some were yet soiled) parishioners were still inside. We started the fire in the electrical outlets. The doors were suddenly bolted shut by some invisible force. We could hear the screaming and clawing at the doors. There were frantic wails calling out to Jesus—who, by the way, never showed up. By the time the fire department arrived, there was nothing left there except the cinder blocks on which it had stood. It was ruled an accidental fire, of course. All of the parishioners attending that night perished, may God rest their souls (wink, wink).

On March 21, 1973, our church celebrated the traditional Wiccan holiday of Ostara. It was the first true day of spring, and the ceremony was very beautiful. The altar was covered in flowers and the entire coven wore flowers in their hair and around their necks and ankles. The ceremony was lengthy in the sense that there was a lot of dialog. The main premise for the holiday celebration is that the daylight and the darkness are of equal length and that the young god is continuing to grow and mature. During the celebration the use of the athame and a priapic wand is necessary. The priapic wand is one in which a phallus is carved into it at one end and is used in any celebration that has to do with procreation, such as this one and the one that followed, the hand-fasting ceremony.

Tara and I met with the other eleven for the hand-fasting ceremony, which was done in our own way—the dark way. We met together at the sacrificing area, near the clothesline. The spring night was mild with a clear sky and the air was perfumed with the smells of roses and other flowers blooming in the flowerbed near the ladies' house. We were all skyclad, and Judex served as priest for the occasion. He erected the temple, opened the circle, and was anointed with the blood of a freshly killed cat by Chakkra, who was standing in as priestess. Tara had a preference for cats, so a cat it was. It was the same anointing as before: the mark of the Celtic cross on the forehead, the pentagram over the left breast and a triangle from the genitals to the right breast and then to the left breast and back to the genitals. He began the ceremony by ringing the bell five times and asked,

"Who has come before the Lord and Lady tonight, the night of Ostara, and to what end?"

"It is I, Tara, who comes as one who wishes to be handfasted," she said from behind the others who were there to witness the event.

"To whom shall you be handfasted?"

"She will be handfasted to Drahcir," I said as I came from the darkness beyond the candlelight. Tara and I walked to the front of the crowd and stood before the priest and priestess.

Judex passed the smaller end of the priapic wand to me, and Tara held the carved end of the wand as we made our vows.

"Tara," Chakkra asked, "do you come to be united with Drahcir on your own free will, to be with him through good times and bad times, through wellness and illness, for as long as your love exists?"

"I do," Tara answered.

"Drahcir," Judex asked, "do you come to be united with Tara on your own free will, to be with her through good times and bad times, through wellness and illness, for as long as your love exists?"

"I do," I answered.

Chakkra then took a cord and tied our left hands together.

"Bring the drink offering—the bowl of binding," Judex instructed.

The bowl was brought out and in it was wine. Judex removed a thorn from a rose stem with the athame and pricked our index fingers on our left hands with the thorn. We each let a drop of our blood fall into the wine. The bowl was then placed on the ground between Tara and me. Tara squatted over the bowl and urinated just a bit into it. When she was finished I also urinated into it.

Judex took the bowl from the ground, held it high over his head, and chanted over it, *"Rex obscurum, tu suscipe pro animabus illis quarum hodie memorium facimus. Obscurum æterna cadant eis, Domine, cum angles tuis in æternum."* (Lord of Darkness, do thou receive them for these souls we commemorate today. Let everlasting darkness fall upon them, O Lord, with thy angels forever.)

Chakkra took some of the drink offering and anointed me with it. Judex did the same to Tara.

"Drahcir, if you take this woman in binding, drink from the bowl," Judex instructed.

I drank.

"Tara, if you take this man in binding, drink from the bowl," Chakkra instructed Tara.

She drank.

"You are now both joined in handfasting for as long as you both shall love, and it is only left for you to consummate the binding before all of your brothers and sisters in the ancient manner as prescribed in the writings."

Chakkra unloosed our ceremonial binding, Tara got on her knees and elbows and amid the applause and approval of the coven I mounted my bride and consummated the binding. We were now officially man and wife. After the ceremony the thirteen of us celebrated in a rousing display of drunken hedonism and debauchery. It was truly glorious.

CHAPTER 12

I n keeping with the custom of the church, Tara and I decided to sleep apart. All the men slept in a different building than the women, so when I got into the trailer later that night I went straight to bed to sleep it off. I had trouble going to sleep, although in the drunken state I was in I should have been able to go to sleep right away. I tossed and turned well into the night. Every time I managed to dose off I had a disturbing dream. Although, I wouldn't say it was actually a nightmare.

I was dreaming of a young woman. She appeared to be a long way from me standing on an expanse. There was nothing over our heads and nothing under our feet. There was light that engulfed us as we stood in the void. She was beckoning me to come closer. I knew who she was, but I couldn't remember her name. She was attractive even though she was a long way off. She was not threatening me in any way, but in a voice that came to me only in waves she was telling me to beware. It was such a chopped up sloppy mess that the last time I awoke I determined myself to go back to sleep and pursue the woman to find out what she was trying to say. The fourth time I went to sleep I contacted the woman.

We were levitating over water. It may have been the Gulf of Mexico or maybe even the Atlantic, but it was a huge expanse of water. There were clouds boiling over our heads and an occasional lightening bolt streamed across the sky. She was dressed in a flowing white gown and her hair was long and as black as a raven. Her full, luscious lips were the color of a magnificent ruby glittering in the sunshine. When I saw the glowing emerald eyes I recognized her; it was Cassandra. I put my guard up as soon as I recognized her, and it shown in my eyes that I was concerned about being there with her.

"You don't have anything to fear from me, Drahcir. I'm not here to do you any harm," she said. Her body and face were outlined in a white light and her movements were as if she was in a strobe light. Her hair was blowing behind her, and her clothing was clinging to her even more than that night we saw her by the river. She didn't seem intent on posing any danger. Her flunky was not even there with her.

"What do you want, Cassandra?" I asked still apprehensive that she may try to lash out at me if I let my guard down.

"I'm here to warn of the impending danger you face, Drahcir. I have been trying to get here to warn you for several days, ever since the night you saw me there on the river bank of your home town, but the angels that Tara sent to stop me are very strong. I have only now been able to call my own angels to over power them."

"What is this supposed danger I am faced with?"

"The woman you have become handfasted with is not who you think she is. She has deceived you from the very beginning. She cast a spell on you to become attracted to her. She put your family under a spell so she could have unlimited access to you. She has led you into a religion that is doomed to failure by posing it as a Wiccan church."

"Judex told me that it was not a true Wiccan church a long time ago. How am I in danger?"

"Everything she does is in a mirror image of things that are done in the bible. She has a chosen few, as Jesus did. She had you to eat and drink before you went into the room you perceived to be the throne room of Satan."

"How do you know about that, and how do you know it wasn't the Lord's holy of holies?"

"To answer the first question let me say that your lady is a very powerful witch, but she is far and away not even close to me. I am a true Wiccan witch. She is a satanic witch. She is of the blackest occult, and it is built on lies. She is not even being considered as the High Wiccan Priestess of North America, like she told you and all of her family. Only those of the true belief fill that position. To answer the second part of your question, I was there. You couldn't see me, but I was there. I have been watching over you from the beginning.

The one you saw as Göndul and the one you saw as Lucifer were some pupils of hers in the occult. She is trying to get an equal position in the satanic craft as High Priestess of North America," she said as the scenery changed. We were now in the desert and the days and nights were flashing by in rapid succession. The sand dunes shifted as if they were crawling about the desert floor like serpents, and the vegetation sprouted, grew and withered in a matter of seconds.

"What about Tyr?" I asked her. "Was that Bragi or Bres?"

"There never was anyone named Tyr. He was an illusion for you to accept to bring you confidence."

"Why would she do all of that? That was too elaborate to go through only to give me confidence in trying to learn witchcraft."

"Are you familiar with any of the Bible at all, Drahcir?"

"I've never sat down and read it exactly. Why would you ask me that?"

"Have you ever heard of the Passover?"

"I'm familiar with the story. It's about when the Jews were slaves in Egypt. The angel of death passed through Egypt killing each first born son in that entire country because Pharaoh wouldn't listen to Moses. All of the Jews put the blood of a lamb on the doorpost and death passed over them. I know that much about it."

"Today," she continued, "the Jews keep the Passover feast by meticulously cleaning the entire house to ensure that there are no bread crumbs in the house. It would desecrate the house to have any yeast in it. The women go to a kosher market and purchase a leg of lamb and the herbs for the feast. Long ago, however, the Hebrews took the Passover more literally as the way it is described in the Torah. In Exodus chapter twelve and beginning at verse five, God is giving instruction to Moses as to how the lamb is to be chosen and cared for before the sacrifice. He says in verses five and six, 'The animals you choose must be…without defect,' and 'Take care of them…all of the people of the community must slaughter them at twilight.' In the true practice of Judaism, as they follow the very letter of the law, the lamb to be sacrificed is not only just cared for, it is treated as one of the family. It eats with the family, travels with the family, and even sleeps with the family. In this way the family holds an emotional attachment to the animal. They love it. When they sacrifice it, they truly sacrifice something they love.

"And so what is it you're trying to tell me?"

Again the scenery changed. We were in the center of an electrical storm. The bolts shot around and through us. The wind was blowing our clothes and screaming across our ears, and yet I was able to hear Cassandra with no problem at all.

"The festival of Beltane is coming," Cassandra continued. "In the Wiccan Church it is the celebration of the fertility of the goddess and the love that the young god brings her. It is a time that the young god makes love to the goddess and the fruits and crops of the earth become ripe. In the Satanic Church, Beltane is celebrated with sacrificing, a feast, and a demonic orgy. On this night it is said that Satan goes about the earth appearing in the covens that has most pleased him. He doesn't have the power God has of being omnipresent, so he appears for only a few minutes, and then he speeds away to the next coven. At each stop he receives either a sacrifice for transference of powers, or he receives sexual favors from a man or woman to the same end, usually for a high priesthood or priesshood. The sexual relations had with Satan are excruciating and can be mortally wounding. It is said that the devil's penis is like that of a cat's—it is barbed."

"So you're trying to tell me that if I'm expected to receive a priesthood I'll have to take a pointy pecker up the old poop shoot? Is that the danger you're trying to warn me about?"

"No, Drahcir. What I'm trying to tell you is that you are the lamb."

The thought was preposterous. The church would never do anything to me. It was ridiculous.

"Are you saying that the coven will kill me on the night of Beltane?"

I thought back quickly on all of the times I poured my emotions out to Sylvia. The many times I told her I loved her, and I couldn't remember a single time she ever said she loved me. There were many endearing things she said, but the words "I love you" were not among them.

Rage was welling up in my chest. It was because I could see that what she was saying could have merit. It could possibly be true. Tara warned me about Cassandra, though. Maybe she was here only to plant doubt in my mind. It would be a good trick. She seemed so sincere talking about my danger. She is only here to railroad me and my relationship with Tara.

"I think you're lying," I told Cassandra. "I think you're trying to scare me out of the fight between you and Tara because your traveler is not as proficient in the Craft as I am."

"The traveler you're referring to is my brother, my real flesh and blood brother. He is not a warrior."

"Why have you been watching over me? If you and Tara are not in competition with each other as the High Priestess of North America why are you both keeping an eye on each other?"

"Tara and I were in school together in New Orleans. We both started learning Wicca at an early age, and we were both very good at it. The sisters were extremely proud of both of us. I continued to learn the Wiccan Craft, but Tara became involved with some of the local voodoo priestesses and those who practiced black magic. She accelerated in the black arts while I accelerated in the Wiccan Craft. The sisters became afraid of Tara and called her the Daughter of Satan. We both graduated at the top of the class. I was number one and she was number two. She has always been against me in everything since then. She wants me out of the way, thinking that she will then be the undisputed top witch in North America in Wicca or Satanism. The only problem with her little plan is that only the Wiccan Witch is recognized as the High Priestess in any position and no other. She believes she can force her way into that position by a sacrifice to Satan."

If she came here with the intent of planting doubt in my mind, she had succeeded. In reflection, there had always been something fishy about Tara. She didn't fit in well with Humble, and I didn't fit in well with her followers.

We now stood in a snow-covered wasteland and several transparent spheres of alternating color were hovering close to us ringing softly, as if they were vibrating. Swirls of soft snow blew around us as we talked.

"There's something in what you are saying that has the ring of truth to it," I admitted to her.

"And do you know why that is, Drahcir? You want to go back to the way you were before all of this happened. You want to hang out with your old buddies and get back to the simple things. You're still a young man. You want to go to college and raise a family in a normal way. You have so many things ahead of you in the future. You don't need a lot of responsibility right now. Look at you. You're handfasted. You have to keep improving in the arts, for her sake. You have people afraid of you when what you really wanted in the first place was for people to respect, or at least just accept you. You want to get back to that time in your life when you were innocent of the ugliness you have had to see. Like everyone else in the world, you want to get back to an age of innocence, a return to an age that is sought in vain. You can never be as innocent as a child again. You can only have a clear conscience."

I paused for a moment and then I said, "I will keep in mind what you told me, Cassandra. If what you have said about Beltane is true, I'm going to find a way to find out."

"I'll help you find those things, Drahcir. My job as a Wiccan is to help those who are in trouble, and you are in big trouble. And you will not be alone with this knowledge. There are others in your coven that are not happy with the direction that Tara has taken. I'll be close, Drahcir."

CHAPTER 13

In the weeks that followed I saw nothing that would lead me to believe that Cassandra was telling the truth. The coven grew closer. I grew stronger. Tara included me in her decisions concerning the coven. She did not, however, include me in her little jaunts to deal with matters of the state. She had to make two trips in the physical mode of transportation since I had gotten involved with the church. The first one she had to go to was in Little Rock to make a decision on a matter concerning the problem of which priestess was next in line to fill the office left vacant by the stepping down of the high priestess of Arkansas. The second time was to attend the funeral of the High Priest of Germany. She was away for a week for that one. She never told me the particulars of the trips she took, only where she had to go and why, and for about the length of time she expected to be away. She never would elaborate on the details of what happened during the trip. She said it was a lot of political crap, and I would just be bored. After hearing what Cassandra had to say, it really bothered me that she wouldn't tell me about the trips. I tried to believe, as I did at first, that she was right. It probably was a lot of political junk. I didn't do politics, anyway. I couldn't even keep up with what Nixon was doing, how could I expect to keep up with all of this other stuff.

I was not the only one who didn't know the ins and outs of Tara's business. No one else in the church knew exactly where she was going or what she was doing. If anyone were to know, anyway, it would have been me.

In the weeks following the wedding she made two more trips. The first trip was to hold an emergency meeting of the cabinet, or so I was told.

"What do you mean by a cabinet? You never mentioned that before," I asked her.

"Oh, Drahcir, you know I have the responsibility of the entire US right now, and that involves the cooperation of many of us. It's not a dictatorship, you know."

"Where is it going to be held? How long will you be gone? Is there any reason I can't go with you?"

"The meeting is held in the capital, Denver, where I'll be for about a week. I'll be meeting with the cabinet the entire time I'm there, and you'll just be bored. Really, it's just the political aspects of the Craft. B-o-r-i-n-g, you know what I mean? Don't worry. I'll come see you every night."

I was getting pretty good at astral projection, but I was not quite able to get all the way to Denver. I gave her the benefit of a doubt. She went. She was gone for not quite a week, and when she got back she didn't talk about what went on. She didn't even mention the names of anyone that was there with her, not that I would have known them.

The second time she said she had to go, she said it was a meeting with the head witch of Canada. My patience was getting very thin by now. This happened on April 27th.

"Why do you need to see the head witch of Canada?" I asked. I was not letting my imagination run away. I was trying to keep myself cool.

"Baby, it's political stuff. How many times do I have to tell you? The Canadian and US ambassadors to the UN are undecided on a particular resolution that the Soviet Union is proposing. The resolution has to do with establishing Soviet military bases in Afghanistan, and the Canadians and the US want the Soviets to allow concessions in our favor."

"How does that effect you personally?"

"The UN ambassadors want us to manipulate the Soviets to see things our way."

I couldn't handle it anymore. "Bullshit!" I declared as I slammed my fist down on the table. "Where are you going, Tara? Do you have some other little traveler on the side somewhere? Were you raised in such an environment that you place no value on your family? Do you think I am so damn gullible that I'm going to swallow everything you tell me? I am your family now. I am your husband, and as such, I am the head of this household. There *are* going to be some changes. I am going to have the say so between you and me. You are going to quit trotting off to B.F.F. every two or three weeks, and when you are required to go, I will go with you. I will be included in the goings on of whatever it is you are involved with. Do you understand what I am saying?"

There is calm before any storm that should be relished whenever possible, for as long as possible. The calm preceded this hurricane and was followed closely by the room literally exploding, and the concussion that ripped the doors and windows out of their frames was ear splitting. In the room where we were standing the furniture was scattered and some pieces were broken. It dislodged all of the loose objects in the room and on the walls. Glass and bits of wood went flying through the air and the impact on my ears was as painful as any punch I had taken on the side of my head. I was certain that a bomb had just exploded within the trailer. That's what I thought until I saw the look in Sylvia's eyes. They were huge and protruding from the sockets. I had never seen a look of pure rage like she was showing me at that moment. Every vein in her head was bulging to the point it looked like she could have had a stroke any second. Her nostrils were flared, and her ears were actually pulled back against her head. She bared her teeth. The canines were growing long and her back was arching making her appear to be growing very big. The time to depart had clearly passed me by. I was in the hands of the maddest witch on earth.

"What part of I am royalty didn't you understand when we first started dating, numb nuts? I am your High Priestess, and you are an insignificant common rookie witch. You will do what I say you'll do, and you'll do it and be glad you're doing it. You will be honored to be handfasted to me and the decisions about running this country, this coven, and this family will be mine and mine alone. Those decisions will not be disputed or questioned. Is anything I have said to you unclear in any way?"

Oh, if I could only have been a little wiser and just nodded in agreement with her. How wonderful life would have been. Perhaps the sun would have appeared and the birds may have begun to sing. Would daisies have appeared, I wonder? Oh, but, no, the male pride welled up in my chest, and at that point, I opened my mouth and allowed my stupidity to hang out there in front of God and everybody.

I began to shape shift also, as pathetic an attempt as it was. I tried to shift into the shape of a wolf, but I really felt it came out looking more like some stupid baboon. I even felt like I had a big old honking, nasty looking ass hanging out behind me.

"Don't try to cloud the issue with the crap about royalty. There is no position available to you. It's all been a lie. Your whole life is a lie. Our relationship has been a lie. The very foundation of your homemade church around here is just one big lie. You don't love me. You've never said you love me. You're just using me to get the recognition from your Lord."

"Who told you that shit? I haven't lied to you about anything. What do you mean I'm using you?" Her form was altering further into the form of a cat. The nose that was only flared a moment ago began to show signs of whiskers coming from the sides and her voice was becoming horribly screechy.

"I just think you want me to do good for you so the master will see what a good teacher you are and give you some sort of promotion," I began to stutter just a little, and I could not hold the shape any longer. I reverted back to my own shape. That is when she knew that I knew things were really not what they appeared.

"Oh, I see," she snarled. "Me thinkth thou hast consorted with familiar spirits." Claws came from her fingers and her voice was becoming almost inaudibly screechy. She held out her clawed hand and slowly closed her fist squeezing my balls, telepathically, from fifteen feet away. The pain was intense, but I could feel she was prepared to squeeze as hard as she needed to get the answers she wanted. "Drahcir, my pet, have you been talking with my dear sister, Cassandra?"

114

I was grimacing and drops of sweat were beginning to run down my face. "Cassandra?" She tightened her grip. I was on tip toe, as if that was going to relieve any of the pain.

"She came to me in a dream telling me a bunch of garbage that I knew wasn't true. She said if I stayed I would have to let the devil screw me up the butt so you could get the promotion you were wanting. I knew she was lying."

"So why didn't you tell me she was seeing you, my love?" she asked as she shook my balls around just for the hell of it. "Did you believe her enough to get into her knickers, you whore? Did you and the nymph of New Orleans have a nice little fuck on the ethereal plane? You might as well have. Every swinging dick in the French Quarter had a good time with her." Her grip tightened a little bit more. "Did you screw her?"

"We didn't do anything but talk," I finally broke down with the tears of pain rolling down my cheeks. "Let me go. Don't hurt me anymore," I begged. The pain was so excruciating, I would have done anything to be free of it.

"You lying little bastard, she spilled her guts about everything. I suppose she also told you that everyone has been working your magic for you to build up your confidence. The truth of that is you couldn't magic your way out of a paper bag. You're going to stay right here until I get back." She forced me to open my mouth and to swallow a capsule of some sort. "You're not going anywhere." And with a final squeeze of my nuts that I thought would crush them she let me go. I probably would have felt quite relieved except that I passed out. What she did and where she went after that was unknown to me. I was oblivious to everything until I woke up three days later.

When I regained some consciousness, I found myself in the temple. It was a corner of it, anyway, but I could only see at best seventy-five percent of the interior. The part I couldn't see was under some sort of renovation. I heard hammering, sawing, and talking. The voices were those of Judex and his dad, Ogma, and the handyman, Jimmy. Judex's voice was the loudest. Then I saw why it was the loudest. He was squatting down beside me smacking me in the face.

"Drahcir. Drahcir, can you hear me?"

I heard only pieces of their conversation. I couldn't focus on anything. It was like everything was fragmented, it was like I was trapped in a nightmare. I heard Judex saying, "How did you come up with that wild story, dad? No one would ever believe that."

"It doesn't really matter if anyone believes it, boy. It will buy us some time."

Jimmy came and looked at me once. His face looked huge as he bent down to look at me. "She sure messed this boy up. When she supposed to be back from Australia?"

I was fading in and out constantly until later that evening. Whatever it was that I was on began to wear off. I remember thinking, *Don wouldn't like this shit, at all. It probably wouldn't go very well with a Tequila Sunrise.*

The next thing I was aware of was Tara's mother, Isadora, was washing my face with a washcloth. She had brought me into the house and was taking care of me. Everyone else was gone.

"What happened?" I asked.

"You went up against the Daughter and lost, sweetie."

"Was it true what she said about everyone working my magic for me?"

"I'm afraid it was, honey. She deceived you just as she deceived all of us."

"How do you know she did? How did you find out?"

"The day after you had your little squabble with her, Cassandra came to Chakkra. After they confirmed with each other that Cassandra was there under a white flag she explained to Chakkra everything about Tara. Of coarse, Chakkra didn't believe her at first, but then she realized that everything she was being told had the ring of truth about it. Cassandra even told Chakkra about the time that she was with Tara in New Orleans and they were walking along the Rue de Chartres late one night, and they were both quite drunk. This was during the time when they were still friends and not yet mature witches.

As they walked along the Rue de Chartres they came to the old building known as the Ursaline Convent. The legend of the convent is a very old one because the building is one of the oldest buildings in North America. It was built by men that had been prisoners in France, but they were offered the opportunity to go to New Orleans to serve their time there. I suppose they figured it was better than rotting in the Bastille. Anyway, the volunteer workers grew restless because they didn't have a way to satisfy their natural urges. A few tried to runaway through the swamps that surround New Orleans to find some Indian girl to sleep with. But, there were two things wrong with that plan. Number one: those swamps are full of hungry gators, and number two: Indian daddies didn't like these guys trying to kidnap their daughters. So, many, if not all of the guys that tried to escape, met a sad fate in the swamps. So the French soldiers came up with a plan. They would get volunteer women out of the French women's prison to come and service these men. They had all types of women in there, thieves, whores, killers….all of the worst elements of French society. The women were given wooden chests to pack their few possessions in. The chests were long and narrow, and they became very practical because while the women were making the crossing across the ocean many of them died. The chests were just the right size to put the bodies in for burial. About half of the women made the trip all the way in to New Orleans without succumbing to some sort of disease. Those that didn't were covered with lime to slow down decomposition. However, when the ship docked there were several on board who were sick and were not allowed to go ashore. They died while on the ship, and it was unclear where they and the others should be buried because there is a problem with burying a body in New Orleans—it comes back up out of the ground. The city is below sea level and the ground water forces the bodies back up to surface. So, it was decided that the women's bodies would be stored on the top floor of the convent until such time as they could be properly buried. The bodies were placed on the top floor and within a few nights strange things began to happen in the French Quarter. People began to die from blood loss. They were totally drained of blood, which is almost impossible to do and no one has explained it, but they had no blood in them. Soon it was suspected that the bodies in the convent were rising from the dead and coming into the streets to find their victims. As a means of defense the people asked the bishop to bless four thousand nails with which they sealed the shutters on the top floor windows hoping to prevent the vampires from escaping. It apparently didn't work. As Tara and Cassandra passed in front of the convent that night two women took hold of them and brought them into the convent. As witches, they tried to fight them off, but the women were too strong for them. They identified themselves as Succubus Witches. They made a deal with Tara that if she would supply them with a toy, she and Cassandra could go free. Tara agreed to do that. She told them that she had a brother that would serve their purposes. So, she betrayed Bruce to the witches of the Ursaline Convent that night. As a means of insurance, the witch bit Tara on the back left shoulder blade and drew blood. She told Tara that if she failed to fulfill her promise she would be brought back to the convent to remain with them as a vampire. For years Bruce was tormented by a reoccurring dream that many women were seducing him. It was draining him physically and emotionally. Chakkra realized it was a succubus and performed a spell to prevent them from attacking him anymore. He almost died from it. Don't you see, sweetie? If she would sell out her own brother, she'd sell out anyone."

I heard what she was saying, but I was still rather groggy from the mickey from which I was just now sobering up. The room was still spinning.

"So, does Cassandra know if Tara has become a vampire because she's not able to keep up her end of the deal?" I asked Isadora.

"All we know is that Tara *did* provide a victim. She fulfilled her end of the bargain."

The words were floating in my head. I didn't want to believe them. I still loved Tara. She couldn't be a monster. She wouldn't do any of the things people have said she has. If I apologize to her everything will be all right. We can go back to the way we started out. I know we can.

"Where is she? I have to apologize. I was wrong and I need to make up with her. Where is Tara?"

"You just lay here. We have everything under control."

"I have to apologize. I have to apologize," I kept saying as I went under again.

When I came to, I was in the temple lying naked on my back on top of a cross. My ankles were tied, and it seemed unusually dark. There were new drapes, black, of course. There was even a black curtain covering the ceiling. The torches did little to illuminate the room and the same was true of the candles that were sitting on the tall brass candelabras. The giant goat's head at the front of the altar was the one thing that seemed to glow. The eyes were made of red faceted glass.

I heard Tara's voice to my left, and I saw her standing in the front of the altar. She was anointing herself. It struck me as odd because I had never heard of anyone anointing themself. She was wearing the pentagram, the Sephiroth ring and her goddess crown. It was not normal for her to be wearing the crown or the ring. She didn't wear them at any common festival. She said she wore them only at special ceremonies. The crown was made of gold, and it was beautifully adored with a crescent moon on the front. The Sephiroth ring was made to represent the tree of emanations from the Kabbalah. It had ten limbs on the tree and each one had a different colored gem on it.

I saw the rest of the coven to my right. They too, were skyclad and seemed to have a strange look on their faces. I saw Judex. He had a look of determination, as did his father, and Isadora was remaining calm.

Tara was chanting a prayer, and I knew I had heard it before. It was similar to the prayer she offered to Damballah on the night we prayed for me to become more powerful, the night we sacrificed the first dog. After she prayed, she held up three golden spikes, a large hammer, and then she held up a spear and after each she asked a blessing on it. After each blessing she rang the bell three times.

Into the chalice, which was on the altar, she poured the wine as a drink offering and prayed. Then she repeated the same as she poured in water for purity. After that, she cut her left palm and let the blood drip into it representing her life force sacrifice. Finally she set it on the ground, squatted over it and urinated into it. The urine was to exemplify the dead returning to life. When the mixture was complete she held it up to the goat's head/pentagram, chanted a prayer to the master, and drank the contents of the chalice. She was becoming more absorbed in this ritual more than any other I had ever witnessed. She was totally animated as she danced around the altar in a filthy, disgusting manner. She cavorted around the entire parameter in dance.

When she came back to the altar, she ordered Judex to step forward. He came and she gave him the spikes and the hammer. He sat one spike at my feet and one at my right hand the last one he held as he stood over me at my left side.

"In the tradition as set by you, my lord," she prayed to the goat's head. "As you pierced, degraded, and finally killed the great enemy, accept the offering of my sacrifice. Take this blood and give me, your daughter, the power to become your highest handmaiden. Take me, father, and ravage me. Come inside me and take your pleasure."

She turned to Judex to watch as he drove the spike through my left wrist and into the heavy, coarse oaken beam. The anticipation she wore on her face was like a child waiting for her birthday present. In the excitement of the moment she was actually visibly trembling. Judex gripped the spike in his left hand and the hammer in his right hand and looked down at me with a wink. I glanced up at him and then back to Sylvia, who was beginning to masturbate on the altar. "Do it. Do it." She was moaning. I wasn't really sure if she was telling her brother to nail me or if she was telling the devil to come nail her.

And then, in the most blatant act of defiance I have ever seen from Judex, he threw down the hammer and the spike. I was so busy trying to make sense of what he had just done everything—time, movement, speech—slowed to a crawl. When the tools finally hit the ground there was a silence that could be felt throughout the temple. Judex was staring at his sister, inviting the displeasure he knew she would be exhibiting in only a matter of seconds.

With the eyes of one who was truly insane, Tara flipped her hand and the spike stood upright over my right wrist, and the hammer was drawing back to strike, when Tara was knocked off of her feet and slammed into the wall several feet away. I looked and saw Chakkra and Judex attacking Tara, metaphysically, to prevent her from doing me anymore harm. Their determination was evident on their faces as they continued to hold Tara to the wall.

The faces of Osix and Isadora were contorted as they fled the sanctuary weeping. Isadora was being hurriedly helped out by Osix, as she was crying and reaching with outstretched arms for Tara, her baby. I turned to the other members, who were showing signs of surprise and of joy. They too, began to attack her with witchcraft, venting their anger at the report they had heard from Cassandra. Those who attacked her were still not without fear of her, and some had already begun to run away when Tara unleashed a fury that even I had not experienced.

She screamed an unearthly howl, and her skin was crawling around on her bones as she mutated into her form of choice, that of a cat. The hair she was manifesting on her body was standing on end and saliva dripped steadily from her mouth as she moaned in a feline fashion. The concussion of the blast she manifested knocked everyone in the temple flat on the ground. The torches fell to the ground and ignited the drapery, which was all over the temple. Sylvia had instantly shifted into the cat and was crouching to attack her rebellious brother when a flash of light, like lightening, appeared over the place she was standing. In an aura of white light, Cassandra appeared and was ready to take on the wrath of the devil's own daughter.

"You bitch!" Tara screamed at her rival. "You're the one who caused all of this. I will make you to suffer a slow painful death."

She flew up at Cassandra and as she came close she was knocked away screaming obscenities as she fell. She then tried to scratch Cassandra from across the room. Cassandra repelled the attack and Tara's efforts were all in vain.

"I told you several weeks ago that I wasn't ready," Cassandra told Tara. "But, I have gotten much, much stronger since then. And speaking of bitches..." she said, and then she threw Tara down to the ground. A cloud of dust arose from the floor of the barn, which mingled with the gathering smoke. Flames were now spreading throughout the barn and the remainder of the coven who had been helping Cassandra began to unceremoniously dismiss themselves. Tara's parents had been among the first to leave. As she struggled to shake the cobwebs from her head, Tara was transformed back to her earthly form and was standing gazing up at Cassandra. She tried to attack her again by invoking demons to throw her to the ground too. The best Tara's little helpers could muster was to knock Cassandra against a wall. As she was pinned to the wall Tara levitated a spike and as just as quickly as a dart, it was racing for Cassandra's head. With wild, confident eyes Cassandra transformed the projectile into a harmless puff of smoke. Seeing that Cassandra was standing in just the right spot, Tara willed the giant pentagram down while laughing maniacally. As it fell onto her, Cassandra changed it to become a sparkling mist and disappear. Then she was up again, high in the air over Tara. Cassandra twirled her finger in the air over her and set the black witch spinning wildly, and as she was spinning she burst into flames and began screaming. She burned in a white-hot flame, fire too bright to look at with the naked eye. It was as bright as daylight inside the burning temple. She burned until there was nothing left of her.

The barn was now fully engulfed in flame. Judex cut the rope off of my ankles, and everyone that was left ran from the burning building. Cassandra hovered over the property and ignited the other buildings, the house and the trailers. Then she was gone. As I looked around, everyone was gone—all of the coven members—the Chase's—everyone. There was no one left, except Jimmy. I didn't linger there to talk to him. The wail of sirens was already audible above the crackling fires.

I sat in my bedroom on the morning of May 1, 1973, and listened as the rest of Humble and the world, learned of the schizophrenic cult members that had been nested in a little country town twenty miles north of Houston. The reporter said that a grounds keeper was instructed by Mr. Chase, the property owner, to set fire to the buildings as the family made their way to Australia. The reason for the abrupt exodus—the property owner said that the United States was to be invaded by Mars in the very near future. According the helper, Mr. Chase had been in contact with the martians for several years and the invasion was imminent.

Epil⊕gue

This rendition of the story is at least the way I remember it to the best of my ability. The groundskeeper admitted to the press that he had set fire to the buildings. The family members instructed him to explain to the authorities that they had made a hurried exodus of the country to relocate in Australia, and they gave him instructions on what to say the reason was that he torched the property. The reason he gave was that there was to be an invasion by Mars in the near future.

The reason for the partially unearthed animal graves, the true purpose for the large hooks on the clothesline, and the assorted, mysterious chemicals found in the ruins of the shed near the clothes line, were never truly known to the outside world. Speculation had it that the animals had been brutally mutilated and sacrificed. Whatever the reason there was for these things that were found in the ruins of the property will never truly be known to anyone outside of the "family."

After the news of the story broke, a mob from the city of Humble turned out at the burned out ruins to gawk at whatever there was to see. My mother took my sister, my brother, my friend Don Cox, and me out to see the sight. As the reality of my world had suddenly shattered into a thousand fragments, the only thing I clearly remember seeing was the clothes line with the big meat hooks on it, and the little shallow graves with the cold, dead limbs of animals exposed to daylight with an unknown gelatinous substance on the carcasses. The newspapers declared that the carcasses were apparently hastily buried.

Today, ironically, a United Pentecostal Church stands in the spot where the family's house had been. There has been no invasion of the United States by Mars that we are aware of, and Humble is no longer a small town made up primarily of family members. Houses and places of business line Highway 59 all the way from Houston to Humble. Humble has an impressive mall, and there are restaurants of assorted cuisines all over the sprawling town. Schools, parks, baseball fields, and golf courses adorn Humble making it seem more suburban than rural. It has a fair share of crime, both civil and criminal, to the dismay of the old-timers still living in the area. The artesian well flows perpetually, albeit, somewhat restrained, and drilling for oil is all but dead.

The mysterious, cultish family did leave Humble in a hurry, but it is not truly known if they ever moved to Australia as the reporters stated. It's not known precisely to where they moved.

Printed in the United States
49943LVS00003B/25-27